Shopaholic

JUDY WAITE

ATHENEUM BOOKS FOR YOUNG READERS
New York   London   Toronto   Sydney   Singapore

Atheneum Books for Young Readers
An imprint of Simon & Schuster Children's Publishing Division
1230 Avenue of the Americas, New York, New York 10020
This book is a work of fiction. Names, characters, places, and incidents
are either products of the author's imagination or are used fictitiously.
Any resemblance to actual events or locales or persons, living or dead,
is entirely coincidental.

Book design by O'Lanso Gabbidon
The text of this book is set in Cheltenham.
Printed in the United States of America
First Edition

10 9 8 7 6 5 4 3 2 1

Library of Congress Cataloging-in-Publication Data
Waite, Judy.
Shopaholic / Judy Waite.—1st. ed.
p. cm.
Summary: Tired of household responsibilities and her mother's depres-
sion, Taylor allows a new friend to persuade her to buy things she can't
afford, but she soon discovers that Kat has even more secrets than she
has.
ISBN 0-689-85138-3
[1. Friendship—Fiction. 2. Shopping—Fiction. 3. Stealing—Fiction.
4. Family problems—Fiction. 5. Grief—Fiction.] I. Title.
PZ7.W13325 Sh 2003
[Fic]—dc21   2002026246

For Rachel and Libby

ACKNOWLEDGMENTS

A very special thanks to Liz Cross, my editor at OUP, who has given me endless support and encouragement. Liz kept believing this book would work even—or maybe especially—on the days when I stopped believing in myself.

I t's Christmas day.

Taylor opens the small brown parcel that came in the post yesterday morning.

It's a box—a jewellery box—decorated with twinkling sequined stars. For a moment Taylor feels a wave of panic. She's sure it has been sent by someone who wants to upset her—someone who's guessed the truth. And then she sees Grandad's signature scrawled on the bottom in swirly blue ink and the panic slips back between the rocks again. Instead she makes herself think about Grandad carving the star box, glueing on the sequins, putting everything together and making it special.

Taylor opens the star box. It is full of money—notes and pound coins that, against the sea-green lining, look like treasure. She counts it carefully. Thirty quid. Taylor thinks that thirty quid is loads more than Grandad can really afford. She puts the money into the fluffy tiger-striped purse she's already unwrapped from Sam. Sam is one of Taylor's best mates—she's equal with Sophie. The three of them have all been friends forever—right since playschool days.

Taylor presses the purse against her cheek, and thinks about Sam and Sophie. Lots of things in her life are all screwed up at the moment, but at least she's got them. At-least they're sticking with her.

She puts the purse on the coffee table, next to a pad of "Disco Queen" notepaper that came from Sophie. Then she opens a packet of "Fizzy Fun Bath Crystals," a bag of toffee fudge, and a pair of reindeer ankle socks. One of the reindeer ankle socks plays a tune. It jingles out "Rudolph the Red-Nosed Reindeer" in thin tinny notes.

Taylor puts the star box in the centre of all the presents, fussing with the position until she gets it right. The wintry sun spills in through the window. It lights up the star box and the sequins glow like something magical. Taylor thinks that she'll use Grandad's money to buy herself the "Magic Pens" set that she saw in the art shop window. She wants to choose something that he would like.

It is still early.

Taylor wants to ring Sam or Sophie, but she gets a picture of them both, sitting round Christmas trees. They have presents flying between them and their families in a wild, jazzed-up version of pass-the-parcel. She'll have to wait.

She doesn't race upstairs to tell Mum about Grandad's money.

Mum didn't give Taylor anything. She didn't mention Christmas when Taylor took her a cup of tea in bed. And she isn't up yet.

Taylor turns the telly on. It's *Cinderella on Ice.* Taylor thinks she's a bit past fairy tales, but it's better than nothing. As Cinderella swirls about in her dress of rags, Taylor doodles on the back of Grandad's brown wrapping paper. She sketches a carriage pulled by six white horses. It looks okay until she tries to add the Cinderella. The eyes are huge. Haunted. More like someone on their way to a funeral than a ball. She prints a title underneath the sketch, "Dancing with Darkness," folds the paper into small neat squares, and drops it in the bin.

Then she lets herself ring Sam. "I got thirty quid," she says.

In the background Taylor hears the snap of a cracker. Somebody is laughing.

"That's wild." Sam's voice is bubbly. "I got dosh too. And Sophie did. We're going shopping the day after tomorrow. We're hitting the sales—we want stuff for the next school disco. Are you coming?"

Taylor feels a stab in her stomach. She wonders if Sam phoned Sophie. Or did Sophie phone Sam? Whatever it is, it doesn't matter. The thought that flashes across her head like demented Christmas tree lights is that neither of them phoned her. She wishes she could tell Sam she's busy. Her long-lost cousin who's really a famous pop star has invited her to the studio where he's making his next video. But she knows she'll be sorry two seconds after she's said it. She winds the phone wire tight round her finger. The Magic Pens set is already doing a disappearing trick. "I'll try," she says.

Sam is still fizzy bright. "We're meeting outside Supa Shoppa at ten thirty. We'll walk to Tillingham Shopping Precinct from there. Do you . . ." There's an explosion of noise and Sam gives a sudden squeal. "Hang on. My pig-faced brother's just exploded a party popper next to my ear." She giggles.

Taylor thinks of Sam draped with coloured streamers. In the background she hears Sam's dad singing "I saw Mummy Kissing Santa Claus." Her mum is laughing. Sam's voice comes sparkling back again. "Sorry about that. You still there?"

"Yes." Taylor winds the phone wire tighter. She notices that it only takes a moment for the tip of her finger to turn blue. "Shall I call you tomorrow?"

"We're out tomorrow. A party at my cousin's. Just turn up if you're coming. I've got to run now. I'm about to be force-fed Christmas nosh."

"Okay then." Taylor makes her voice sound as if it's dancing. "Happy Christmas."

"And you."

Taylor stands for a moment, untangling her finger while the line drones its dead flat tone.

Taylor wishes Grandad was here. He almost came. They'd planned it. But he rang in the week to say that Betsy—his ancient heap of a car—was playing up. He couldn't get it fixed because all the garages were closed for the holiday.

She stares down at a stash of papers that have been piling up beside the telephone. It's mainly Christmas cards, a few leaflets and brochures, and a "Spend Spend Spend" plastic credit card that Mum sent off for months ago. Taylor will sort through it all later, keeping the bits that have good colours and interesting textures. She has a box of stuff like this under her bed, but she can't face going through it now.

She wanders into the kitchen.

She's cooking a chicken for her and Mum. She has to get started on it.

She picks out six potatoes from the vegetable basket, and runs them under the tap. The water dances out, all silvery and tinsel bright. Taylor keeps it running for a long time, staring out of the window. It's a nice day for December. Blue sky. Yellow sun. Like a kid's painting.

Taylor gets a sudden picture in her head. It's a little girl with blonde curly hair sitting on the beach. She's got her back to Taylor. She's built a sandcastle and is busy digging out the moat. Beside her is a blue blow-up boat printed with prancing white sea horses. A rainbow-striped rabbit lies nearby, half buried in the sand. The whole scene has a haze round it, ice-cream pink. All sugar-sweet and happy and once-upon-a-time.

"Taylor?"

Taylor turns round.

Mum is standing in the doorway, her shoulders hunched, her dressing gown pulled tight round her as if she's battling against an icy wind.

Taylor nods at Mum. "You okay?"

"I had a terrible dream." Mum sighs and yawns. "Have you been all right this morning? I can't get my head round it being Christmas. We . . . we agreed not to bother with it, didn't we?"

"Yep." Taylor hesitates. It's hard not to bother with Christmas. It's been in her face for weeks. It's easier for Mum not to bother, because she never goes anywhere. But Taylor thinks that's how it should be. She wants to keep things easy for Mum. "I might go out on Tuesday. Shopping. We're going to the sales."

"That sounds nice." Mum passes her hand across her forehead. "I'm exhausted. I have to go and sit down. I just can't seem to shake this off."

Taylor watches Mum drift away into the next room. Mum has a greyness that hovers round her. It hasn't always been there. It wasn't there when Laura was alive. But now Laura is gone, and the greyness never goes away. Taylor sees the greyness as a kind of smudge. It's as if Mum is drawn in charcoal, and some-one has blurred the edges.

Taylor turns back towards the window.

She wants to pull the little girl with the sandcastle back into her head. She wants the ice-cream-pink world again. But when she tries to make the picture it won't come.

A new one builds instead, all creased and muddled, like old summer postcards that have been torn up and scattered. There are ragged corners of sand and sea. There are scraps of castle. Close to the water's edge lies a rainbow-striped rabbit. The tide is coming in.

Taylor sees Sam and Sophie before they see her.

"Hiya!" She puts on her "great to see you" grin. And it *is* great to see them. It's great to be out.

They turn and grin back at her. Taylor sees, with a feeling like a punch in the stomach, that they are wearing lipstick. It's a sort of glossy lilac stuff. Taylor's grin stiffens. She's never worn lipstick. Or at least, only in school plays and stuff. Not proper going-out lipstick. She thinks that they should have told her. Rung her up. "By the way—we're wearing lipstick," they should have said.

Even as Taylor runs it through her mind it sounds stupid. But it matters.

"It's really wild that you came." Sam squeezes Taylor's arm. Taylor realizes Sam's done her hair up too, all sprinkled with silver glitter that sparkles against the liquorice black.

"We're going to have *such* a laugh." Sophie's hair—also

dark, but with reddish tints—is done the same as Sam's. Except instead hers is sprayed with a glittery gold.

They're both wearing skimpy tops and silky black trousers.

Taylor twizzles a stand of her own mouse-brown hair between her fingers. Her hair is boring. Long and straight. The way she's had it since she was little. She feels grubby in her old coat too. It's grey and furry. It was a fun thing once. Everyone called it "The Yeti." She used to love it, and it kept her warm.

The grin is making Taylor's jaw ache. "You must be frozen." She tries to say it brightly, as if being frozen would be a kind of treat. She thinks, as she speaks, that it's the sort of thing her mum might say. Or at least the sort of thing she might have said once.

"No," Sam and Sophie answer together. They are looking at her as if she's just landed from another planet.

Taylor thinks about going home.

She sees herself suddenly running off down the road. She won't explain anything. She'll just go, whizzing away, faster than light. She likes the picture of Sam and Sophie staring after her through the cloud of dust she leaves behind, wondering what's going on.

And then she thinks of herself arriving home. There is a pile of ironing. A vacuum cleaner. A door laced with cobwebs.

Taylor feels a decision harden inside her. This is her being stupid, not Sam and Sophie.

This being left out stuff is all in her head.

She scribbles a line through the "home" picture with an imaginary felt pen, and tilts her chin. "You both look great," she says. "Let's get going."

Tillingham Precinct is buzzing. Taylor has never seen it so busy.

Sophie links her arm. Sam grabs her on the other side. They weave their way through the bustle of people.

Taylor likes having her arms linked with Sam and Sophie. It's as if they're joined together. Siamese triplets.

"Christ. Look at that." Sophie stops suddenly by the fountain in the middle of the square. Beside it there is a Christmas display. It is Cinderella sitting and sewing, surrounded by mechanical mice. There's a Fairy God-mother hovering behind her—all lit up with yellow light—and cotton-wool snow falling outside a painted lattice window. Every ten seconds Cinderella's head tilts slightly, and she reaches down to touch the whiskers of the nearest mouse.

Sophie whirls a penny into the pool of water beneath the fountain. "That Fairy Godmother thing is *scary*. I mean—imagine turning round and seeing her looming up in your front room."

Sam giggles. Her own penny skims the surface. "I bet she scares the pants off all the little kids."

Taylor pushes her hand into her shoulder bag and touches the tiger-striped purse. Then she stops. She's only got Grandad's money in it. She hasn't got any pennies. She pulls her hand back out again, and makes a promise to herself to throw a penny in later. It feels scary not to make a wish.

Mum's voice jumps into her head again. *"Be careful what you wish for, it might come true."* Taylor pushes Mum's words away. She isn't sure what she'd wish for even if she *did* have a penny, but whatever it is Mum won't find out. Or care.

Sophie starts up a high-pitched giggle. "What about Father Christmas? A bloke in a red coat lurking about in your bedroom at night. What kind of a message is *that* for kids?"

Sam starts giggling too. They are both stumbling about, clutching their stomachs, groaning with helpless laughter.

Taylor pulls her mouth into a smile shape. She gets the joke, but she doesn't feel it. She likes the idea of Father Christmas. She likes the Fairy Godmother, too. She's got a big warm face, all crinkly and kind. In fact, Taylor likes the whole scene. She would like to stand for longer watching the head-tilting Cinderella, but Sam and Sophie are pulling her away.

They're both still laughing.

Their laughs have got louder and sillier, and people

are looking at them. Sam and Sophie don't seem to mind. It makes them worse.

Taylor thinks that they never used to laugh like that. They never used to want to make people look at them.

She feels suddenly that they're glowing and golden, bursting out of themselves, like flowers in the sun.

And she's in the shade, caught amongst the cobwebs where the sun doesn't reach.

3

They push their way into Glitzie's.

It is so packed they have to walk sideways, edging past the rows of clothes.

LAST FEW REMAINING.

REDUCED FOR ONE WEEK ONLY.

HURRY WHILE STOCKS LAST.

It's all sparkly. Silky. Sequins. Glitter.

There is an endless throb of pop music. Rikki Cavalier is singing "In the Beginning."

Everyone around Taylor is bright and fast. They rummage through rails. They grab at dresses and jumpers and jackets and skirts. The hangers chatter noisily as they clang together. People push past her. Every now and then something falls to the ground. Nobody picks it up.

Taylor gets squashed against a bin full of "Buy

One—Get One Free" lipsticks, all lilac pinks and deep plummy reds. She wonders if she should get some, although she can't imagine wearing it.

"Look at this." Sophie snatches up a sparkly gold top and holds it against her. "It's only five quid. They're giving it away."

"Wild." Sam leans across her. "I'm going for this silver one. We'll be just *it* for the disco." She begins twisting about in the mirror opposite, holding the top in front of her. Taylor notices Sam has made her mouth go into an odd sort of pout. She's never seen her look like that before.

"And you," says Sophie, turning to Taylor. "Just grab anything. It's all really cheap."

Taylor scans the rails. She can't see anything that she likes. She wonders if she should split away from them. She could go to the art shop instead.

A dress at the end of the rail catches her eye. It's shimmery blue with black straps and tiny glitters of pearl woven into the silk. It has a jacket with it—cobwebby lace—the pearls sparkling through it like frost in sunlight.

There is a ticket clipped to the hanger saying "£19.99." The numbers are big and red, like a kind of shout.

Taylor takes the dress and holds it up.

"That's really special." Sophie bounces over, a Glitzie's

carrier bag swinging from her arm. She has been to pay for the sparkly top. "Have they got any more?"

"It's the only one." Taylor's hand tightens on the hanger.

"Get it quick then. Before someone else does."

Sam appears. She's swinging a Glitzie's bag too. "That's great. Your colour. Stick it on."

They hustle Taylor towards the changing room.

Inside, Taylor takes off the Yeti and hangs it on the hook on the wall. Then she wriggles out of her jumper and jeans, kicks off her trainers, and pulls the dress over her head. This will decide it. She's going to look pathetic. She'll be able to shove the dress back on the rail and race off to the art shop.

"Get on with it. Let's have a look." Sam and Sophie are hovering outside.

Taylor feels stupid. They'll be embarrassed. They won't know what to say. She peers round the curtain, wrapping it round her like a towel. "I don't think . . ."

"Hey. That's wild." Sam grabs the curtain and pulls it wide. She takes Taylor by the shoulders and turns her towards the mirror. "You look older. Taller."

Taylor realizes, with a jolt, that she actually is taller than Sam. They always used to be the same height. It surprises her that her body is growing so fast, all on its own, without her knowing anything about it.

"There's something missing . . ." says Sophie,

wrinkling her nose at Taylor's reindeer ankle socks. "Take those off, and wait there." She's back in minutes, thrusting a pair of black suede shoes with pointed toes and "grown-up" heels through the curtain. "There you go. They're only ten quid."

"They feel like stilts." Taylor totters round the changing room. One heel catches on a discarded reindeer sock. "Rudolph the Red-Nosed Reindeer" starts its tinny tune.

Sam and Sophie link arms. They sway and sing loudly.

The sock slows down and stops at "they never let poor Rudolph."

"You look like a dream," grins Sam. "Now you *shall* go to the ball."

Taylor starts to feel her tummy go knotty. The Magic Pens jump back into her head again, flashing like tiny beacons. She wants to put the dress back and go away and think about it—but suppose it's not there if she decides she wants it? Her throat is dry. "It'll be all my money gone. I'll only have a penny left."

"So what? It's your Christmas money. You're *supposed* to be spending it." Sophie takes Taylor's hair and gently splays it between her fingers. She lets it tumble back down over Taylor's shoulders.

Taylor can't pull her eyes away from the mirror. "It'll need dry cleaning."

"Maybe not." Sam shrugs. "You won't wear it much. We only have a disco once a term, and you'll want something else by the summer."

Taylor runs her gaze across the dress. She wishes she could wear it loads and loads of times. Even at home, just sitting around, it would feel special. She could float about like some princess in a fairy tale, her hair crimped and curled and tumbling around her shoulders.

Sam cuts into her thoughts. "You look great. Really wild."

Taylor lets her hands follow the shape of the dress. It is ice cool against her skin. She thinks of a burst of cold air. Everything blowing clean.

And suddenly she *does* feel great. She *does* feel wild.

"Stick this on too." Sam shakes the cobwebby jacket from the hanger and hands it to Taylor.

Taylor slips into it. Now she is a supermodel. A pop star. Someone collecting a film award. She twists sideways to get a back view in the mirror. She feels flushed and excited. She can't stop giggling. The giggle grows. The sound she makes seems floppy and loose, like the groans of Sam and Sophie earlier.

"Go for it," says Sophie.

"It's too good to miss," adds Sam.

Taylor has one final panic. What if the colour's wrong when she takes it outside? What if she grows even taller? What if she catches the cobwebby jacket on a door handle at home? What if . . .

But though a scramble of doubts twists through her head, her heart is telling her something different. Her heart is telling her she has to have this dress more than anything in the world. "I'm going for it," she says.

4

The queue stretches back out through the door.

It's mainly girls—a few Taylor's age but most of them older. They are heaped high with bargains. Taylor thinks they must have wardrobes the size of garages. She's only got the dress and the shoes, but she doesn't care. She holds the dress slightly up and away from her. She doesn't want it crushed.

A girl nudges her in the back. Taylor stiffens, wondering if she's trying to push in. But the girl is smiling. She nods at the dress, and says in a voice that is huskily warm, "I would have gone for that if I'd seen it. Are there any more?"

"This was the last one." Taylor tries to sound casual, smiling awkwardly back at the girl. She knows who she is—although only from a distance. She goes to the same school. She's a couple of years older than Taylor—one of those girls who always has boys hanging round her. Taylor is staggered by the idea that this girl might consider the same dress as her. "I just saw it and grabbed it."

"I don't blame you. It's great. Really different." The girl shakes back her silvery blonde hair and lightly touches the cobwebby jacket.

Taylor wants to say something sparkly and unusual. She wants to prove she's worthy of the dress, but her mind has suddenly become about as interesting as a lumpy mashed potato. She manages a stumbling, "I think everyone should try to be different."

The girl laughs. "But then everyone would be the same."

Taylor laughs too, trying to work out exactly what it was that she said.

The girl's dark—almost black—eyes catch into hers. They are sparkling, but there's an edge of something else. It's as if some new thought is whirling away in the back of the girl's mind.

"Have some gum." The girl waves a packet at Taylor.

Taylor never chews gum. It's the sort of thing Mum makes a fuss about. *Used* to make a fuss about. "Thanks." She takes it, unwrapping it slowly, folding it into her mouth. It's minty. It's buzzy. Taylor feels older.

She grins at the girl.

The girl grins back. "I'm Kat," she says.

"I'm Taylor," says Taylor.

They watch each other for a moment. They are both chewing, their jaws moving at the same time. Taylor imagines them sitting in her bedroom, practising *and one and chew and one and chew.* She struggles to think of something to say. "I like your jacket," she says at last.

"It's ancient." Kat pulls a face.

Taylor worries that she's said the wrong thing. Perhaps she's shown herself up as someone who hasn't got a clue about jackets.

She hopes Kat doesn't comment on the Yeti. Taylor wonders if she should dream up a story about it. *My jacket's ancient too. My aunt gave it to me, and she's visiting us at the moment. It's the only time I ever wear it. Honestly, I wouldn't normally be seen dead . . .*

Then she hates herself. The Yeti's been a sort of friend. She'll have to switch the talk to something else.

Kat's jacket has three silver buttons, and is cut away from the waist. Taylor realizes that her belly is bare, and it's pierced by a small diamond ring. Taylor tries to look as if everyone she knows has rings through their bellies. "Did that hurt?"

"Naw." Kat pulls another face and touches the ring. "I can get yours done for you if you like. My mum does it."

"Thanks." Taylor can't think of what else to say. She can't imagine Kat will even recognize her at school next week.

The queue shuffles forwards.

As she gets to the checkout Sam and Sophie come fizzing up out of the crowd.

"We've come to watch the big moment," says Sam.

"The moment the dress officially belongs to you," adds Sophie. She waves her hands about with a flourish. "Taylor from Tillingham. This dress is your life."

Taylor giggles. She feels fizzy too. It's as if they're all charged with a buzz of energy. They're a gang of three. A shopping gang.

She turns to grin at Kat, but Kat has disappeared.

"That's £29.99, please." A stick-thin girl wearing electric-blue nail varnish takes the dress from Taylor. The pop music seems louder. It dances through Taylor. Her foot is tapping. Her shoulders jiggle. Taylor suddenly imagines they are in a musical. They're all about to burst into song. The stick-thin girl will jump on the counter and do a dance routine. The whole queue will join in, spinning dresses and shoes and bags and knickers high into the air . . .

"Do you want to keep the hanger?" The stick-thin girl glances at Taylor. She is folding the dress, wrapping it in a sheet of pale lilac tissue paper.

"Yes, please." In Taylor's mind now she opens the door to her wardrobe at home, and hooks the hanger over the rail. The dress glows there like something glorious, blocking out faded cardigans and skirts and jumpers that have gone bobbly with too much washing.

The stick-thin girl puts the shoes in a box, one facing one way, and one the other. Then she lifts the lilac package gently and sets it inside a silver carrier bag.

The bag has a gold italic "Glitzie's" streaking across the outside.

Taylor digs her hand inside her shoulder bag.

Her fingers scrape the hard bristles of her hair-brush.

There's a small packet of tissues and, deep in the bottom, the cold hard metal of her front-door key.

Her purse is gone.

5

"Perhaps you dropped it?" Sam and Sophie fluster around her.

"Perhaps." Taylor is trying to think in slow motion. She can remember having the purse when they were outside, by the Cinderella display. She didn't check it after that.

She thinks of a hand—a stranger's hand—ruffling around in her stuff. They must have been quick. They must have known what they were doing.

Sophie grabs Taylor's bag and empties it out onto the counter.

The stick-thin girl's eyes glance over at the next customer, then flick back to Taylor. "Do you want me to put this by for you?"

"I—no thanks." Taylor's voice has a wobble to it. "Perhaps I'll get it tomorrow."

"It's the last day of this special offer. I'll have to put it back on the rail." The stick-thin girl is already taking the lilac package out of the silver bag with the gold italic writing. She unfolds the dress. Taylor notices that she has a broken thumbnail.

Taylor shoves her things back into her bag, and doesn't look up again.

"Shall we go home?" Sam touches Taylor's shoulder.

Sophie threads her arm through Taylor's on the other side. "It's a crap thing to happen. I know just how you feel. I had a whole load of Body Shop stuff nicked once. I'd only put it down for a second."

Taylor doesn't answer, but she feels better. They're true mates. She'll never have another nasty thought about them again. They're like angels from heaven, wrapping blankets of friendship round her. And Taylor, who has been thinking a lot about angels lately, hangs onto their arms and pulls them in closer.

Suddenly she senses Sophie's step falter. Sophie is turning to a rack of "Not to Be Missed Bargains." "Hey— look at those black trousers. They'll be great with our sparkly tops." She glances back at Taylor. "We won't be long. . . ."

"It's okay." Taylor nods and smiles. The angel's wings are being folded away. She feels cold inside, as if the wind is blowing through her.

Sophie is pulling the trousers off the rack like a hyena attacking a corpse. She is chucking a pair at Sam.

Sam slips her arm away from Taylor to catch the trousers. "Why don't you wait outside . . . ?" she says.

"I'll stand by the fountain." Taylor trails out, almost

colliding with a security man in a dark blue uniform who glares at her for a moment, then walks on by.

She sits on the little wall that runs round the edge of the water. Her jaw is aching, tired of chewing. The gum is as tasty as old cardboard now. She wishes she hadn't got it, but she can't take it out. She wouldn't know where to put it.

The scatter of other people's pennies wink up at her through the silvery water of the pool.

Taylor stares at the head-tilting Cinderella, and tries not to think about the penny change she hasn't got.

6

Taylor goes straight upstairs when she gets in.

The first door she passes is Mum's bedroom door. It is shut. Taylor doesn't try to open it.

Mum is in there. Taylor knows this without needing to check. She may still be in bed, or she may be curled up on the floor by the window. It doesn't much matter which. In either case the room will be dark and Mum will have the curtains closed. The second door—the door to Laura's bedroom—is also shut. There is a lace-work of cobwebs on the handle. Taylor keeps the whole house clean—even Mum's bedroom—except for this door handle. These cobwebs are important. They are a way of helping her to keep control of the house. If they're ever broken, she'll know where Mum has been.

Today she is safe. The cobwebs are still there. If anything, they are thicker than before. Taylor moves on past, taking care not to knock them with her bag. She doesn't let herself think about the room on the other side of the cobwebbed door. She doesn't let herself think about Laura.

She pushes through into her own room.

Oscar, a one-eared teddy, is sitting on her bed.

Taylor presses her nose into his fur. Just the smell of him makes her want to cry. She squeezes him tightly—fiercely—then moves him almost angrily to one side. She is like that with Oscar. He makes her feel things she doesn't want to feel. But she wants him near her. She doesn't want to hide him away.

Taylor empties her bag onto the quilt. She has a sudden hope that perhaps the purse might have got wedged somewhere deep and mysterious. Somewhere so unlikely that she would have missed it amongst the push and shove of the shop. She even runs her finger round the edge of the lining. She is looking for clues. A telly programme super-whizz detective-type would find some, of course. He would pull his hand from her bag in triumph, holding a broken electric-blue thumbnail to the light. The stick-thin shop assistant would be tracked down and forced to admit to owning the other half, still conveniently attached to her thumb. The great "Missing Purse Mystery" would be solved. Things on the telly always have tidy endings.

She looks round her room, a kind of gallery of collages she has built up since playschool. Bits of pasta. Scrunched up tissue paper. Soft gold wire. Buttons. Beads. Each picture has a name. "Rainbow Fairy,"

"Funfair," "Wild Horses." She squints at one of her favourites. This is a shark's fin in a tinfoil blue sea. The fin is cut from Monopoly money, and Taylor has printed "Lone Shark" along the curve. She tried to explain it to Sam and Sophie once when they came round, but they just said she was "loopy."

Taylor doesn't want to think about Sam and Sophie. She thinks about Grandad instead.

She sees his big leathered hands working at his old oak desk, making the star box, filling the box with money.

She sees him leaning over the brown parcel, carefully printing her address.

She sees him carry it to the post office to get the stamp.

Suddenly she grabs a pen from the table by the bed, and pulls out a sheet from the Disco Queen notepaper:

Dear Grandad,

Thank you thank you thank you. The star box is brilliant. I've got it in my room. The Christmas money was great too. I got some really special pens from the art shop with it. They're called Magic Pens. Some of them are silver and gold. One writes in glitter. One draws a kind of zigzag pattern with its nib.

Hope you are well and that you had a great Christmas too. See you next Friday, if "Betsy's" all better.

love and kisses,
Taylor xxxx

"Taylor?" Mum is knocking on the door. It is a quiet knock. An "I'll go away if you want me to" knock.

Taylor shoves the letter under her pillow. "What?"

Mum opens the door. She stays leaning against the frame as if she's afraid she might fall. "Had a good day?"

"I had my purse nicked." It surprises Taylor that she is blurting this out. It surprises her that Mum has even asked the question.

"Oh dear." Mum makes it sound as if Taylor is six years old and has just dropped crumbs from the Christmas cake on the floor. She is smiling, but her eyes are foggy.

"I was going to buy a dress."

"That's nice."

Taylor stubs the end of the pen she was writing with onto the palm of her hand. It makes a clicking noise. "It was a really special dress. Ice blue, with this beautiful cobwebby jacket . . ."

Mum looks puzzled suddenly, as if the fog has just cleared. "Did you say a *dress*?"

"Yes." Taylor clicks the pen again. There is a dent in

her skin. Click. Click. Click. Mum is making it sound as if she is describing a pantomime cow outfit or something. "What's wrong with that?"

"I wouldn't have thought a *dress* was really you."

"What is me then?" The words come out hard and round, like pennies dropping in water. Could a dress be "her"? Or a shaggy grey coat? Or reindeer ankle socks? Are Sam and Sophie those sparkly tops? Is Mum her faded beige dressing gown?

"Oh, I don't know." Mum gives a tired laugh. Taylor can tell that the conversation has already become too tangled for her to follow.

There is silence for a moment.

Although it is not quite silence.

Click. Click. Click.

Mum runs her hand across her face, as if she's checking it's all still there. "I'm not sure what we can eat tonight. I haven't cooked anything. I haven't felt up to it. . . ."

"I'll do something in a minute." Taylor spins the pen up into the air. It twizzles as it falls. She and Mum often play this game—the one where Mum was *about* to cook something. The one where Taylor steps in at the last minute to help. Normally the game makes Taylor feel safe. As if everything is normal, really. As if today is just one odd day out of years of everything being all right. Except it's been months and months since Mum last cooked anything.

And today Taylor doesn't feel safe. She feels

churned up and horrible and she wishes all this could be stopped. She struggles for the right words. She is going to say something. She is going to make Mum be different.

And then she makes herself think about why Mum is like she is, and Taylor clamps her mouth shut into a thin tight line.

Mum is already leaving, backing away, letting the door swing slowly shut behind her.

Taylor sinks sideways onto the bed, her arms reaching for Oscar. She finds him, holds him, curling up tight and small.

The reindeer ankle sock starts up from where it left off in Glitzie's.

Taylor stands in the school corridor and stares. She can't believe it. Sam and Sophie have had their hair cut. It's short. Spiky. Glossed with gel. They look as if they've got giant black sea anemones on their heads.

"When did you do that?" Taylor knows her voice sounds shaky, but she can't help it. It's like the lipstick, only worse. A gang of two.

Sam laughs. The short hair suits her. Her eyes seem bigger. She's got cheekbones. "We went on Saturday. Sophie found a really wild photo. She cut it out from *Girl Talk* magazine."

Sophie giggles. She looks good too. Like she's daring. Up for anything. "It's the newest fashion."

"It's great." Taylor locks her mouth into a smile, but her heart feels roughed up. Bruised. It's not that she would have wanted *her* hair like that. Not in a million years. She just wanted to know. One of them should have rung her. Before. After. Anytime. Sometime before today.

But Sam and Sophie aren't noticing Taylor with her locked-up smile and bruised heart. They are being closed in by other girls. Girls Taylor didn't know they even knew. There's a babble of shrieks and giggles.

"That's really great."

"I wish my mum would let me do that."

"What hairdresser did you go to?"

A couple of boys turn up. They are older. They seem to know Sam and Sophie too.

Taylor hangs back as the ever-growing crowd attaches itself around the centres of Sam and Sophie. They make their way noisily along the corridor.

"Hey there." Someone nudges Taylor in the back.

She turns, startled. It's Kat—the girl from Glitzie's. She's got her hair done over with tiny plaits, and she's wearing a sports jacket that is definitely *not* school uniform.

Taylor forces another smile. "Hi."

"How's things?"

"Fine."

Kat gives Taylor a long look. "You don't look fine. You look—gutted."

"No—honestly . . ." Taylor struggles to make her smile brighter. She can't tell Kat how crazy and pathetic she is. She can't tell anyone. She hates herself for even thinking like it. Who else in the world would go to pieces just because their mates got their hair cut?

"It must be being back here then. First day always

sucks." Kat unwraps a packet of gum and hands a piece to Taylor.

Taylor takes it, wondering how to get rid of it when the bell goes. "You're right. It must be that. A stinking first day back." She pushes out a laugh. A silly giggle of sound. It's not true—not for her anyway. She likes school really. She likes the pattern of the day. She likes the feeling that the hours have edges around them. She knows where she has to be and what she is going to be doing next. She doesn't feel like that at weekends and holidays. Weekends and holidays are cold dark tunnels of time that she has to find her way through.

"I bought you something. A present." Kat digs her hand into her pocket.

"For me?" Taylor says it stupidly, her mouth hanging open like a fish.

"I felt bad for you. It was a crap thing, you getting your purse nicked like that." Kat hands Taylor a small parcel wrapped in sparkly foil paper.

Taylor takes it, a new warmth fluttering up from her stomach. "I hadn't realized you were still there. I didn't think you saw."

"I'd zipped off to get some black trousers. They'd just gone out on the rails. I was going to get back in the queue behind you but the next girl wouldn't let me. She said I'd lost my place. I had to go to the end of the queue."

Taylor is only half listening. She is turning the

present over and over in her hand. She hasn't got a clue what it is. It could be a bit of old wood for all she knows. What matters is that Kat, who probably has a zillion and one mates, thought about her. She picks carefully at the paper. She won't tear at it. The beautiful foil wrapping is part of the gift. "Thanks." She holds the present up now—it is lipstick—the words "lilac shimmer" in jazzed-up letters down the side.

"You haven't got that colour, have you?"

Taylor looks at Kat, wondering just for the tiniest shrimp of a moment whether she is having a laugh. But Kat's eyes are troubled, as if this really matters.

"No—no. Not this colour. Nothing like it." Taylor smiles. A real smile this time. "It's brilliant. Thanks."

The bell goes. Kat falls into step beside Taylor. They are chewing in time again. *Step and chew and step and chew.*

Kat touches Taylor's arm. "What are you doing after school?"

Taylor tries to look as if she has loads of choices. "Not sure yet."

"Come into town," says Kat. "We like the same stuff, you and me. We can have a laugh. Just hang about a bit. We don't need to buy anything."

Taylor hesitates. She normally walks home with Sam and Sophie. She hasn't got any money. She hasn't told Mum.

Farther down the corridor she hears a squeal. She

looks round. Two of the older boys have hoisted Sam and Sophie up onto their shoulders. Everyone else is gathered round, gazing up at them. Taylor imagines Sam and Sophie bathed in light. Cameras flashing. Crowds pushing their way into the school, clapping and cheering and following them down the corridors.

"Okay," Taylor says, turning back to Kat again. "I'll meet you by the gate."

Taylor is "hanging about" in Tillingham. She has never "hung about" anywhere before. It seems to involve walking very slowly—sauntering—with no particular sense of where they are headed. Sometimes Taylor forgets about the sauntering and goes too fast. She had never realized it was so hard to move slowly.

Kat has got it just right—lazy, easy. They could be wandering down a country lane admiring the frost on the branches.

Taylor isn't sure why Kat wants her there, though. Kat might just be killing time. Or maybe it's a joke. A dare. Perhaps Kat's zillion and one mates placed bets on whether Taylor would turn up or not.

She shifts the Yeti from one arm to the other. She has carried it all the way from school. The wind was biting, but she didn't care.

"Let's try here." Kat stops suddenly, swiveling on her heel to face a shop window.

Taylor follows—sauntering—behind Kat into Top Marks. Taylor has never been in Top Marks before. She's always thought of it as too posh.

"What do you want to try?"

"What d'you mean?"

"What d'you like the look of?" Kat is scanning the rails of clothes.

"I haven't got any money."

"So what?"

Taylor eyes the blank-faced shop girl standing by the entrance to the changing room. "Won't she mind?" She feels lost suddenly. It's as if she's joined in in the middle of a game and doesn't know the rules.

"'Course not. Gives her something to do. And we've got as much right to try stuff on as anyone else. We could be the daughters of millionaires, for all she knows."

Taylor shifts the Yeti back to the other arm, and glances down at her school uniform. *She won't think that about me,* she thinks.

"Come on. We'll have a laugh." Kat goes over to a line of tops. "Try these. We're allowed four each."

Taylor takes four, and follows—saunters—behind Kat.

The shop girl lights up as they reach her.

Taylor imagines her being switched on, like one of those battery dolls that walk and talk and blink their eyes.

The Walkie Talkie girl hands out plastic tokens with slots in them. "Just round to your left," she says. She blinks very fast, and smiles, as if she knows there is a huge adventure waiting for them. Taylor thinks that Kat was right—the girl was desperate for something to do.

They go round to their left.

It's a big changing room, a row of mirrors down one side. The lighting is hazy and soft. A thin thread of music drifts through from the shop.

And Kat is right for a second time.

It *is* a laugh. Taylor tries on the first top.

"I wish I had your eyes." Kat says this enviously.

Taylor is startled. She can't imagine she has the sort of eyes that anyone else would want. Especially not Kat. "What d'you mean?"

"Look—with this yellow they're all innocent and young—but now . . ." Kat hands her a dark green jumper, and watches her put it on. "With this they go more thoughtful. Mature." Kat says the word *mature* in a grown-up headmistressy voice.

Taylor giggles, switching tops again, watching herself closely in the mirror. She has never seen her eyes change moods like this before. She didn't know it could happen. She remembers Mum talking about the dress: *"It's not really you . . ."* And Taylor decides that Mum is wrong. She can be anyone. She doesn't change the clothes—the clothes change her.

"Hang on—I know what's missing." Kat rummages in

her rucksack and brings out a silky black bag. "Close your eyes."

Taylor closes her eyes. She hears the snap of the silky black bag opening. She hears the clack of pots knocking together. She feels Kat's light touch on her face. "That tickles."

"Trust me. My mum was a model. She taught me all this." Kat works her way round Taylor's face, smoothing across her cheeks, her nose, and forehead. "Just the eyes now. Keep very very still."

Taylor is aware of Kat's breath on her face. The sweet vanilla smell of her. She lets her mind run to Kat's mum. She bets they look alike. Both slight and blonde and with those dark, dark eyes. She dresses Kat's mum in sprayed-on jeans and a red suede jacket. She probably goes to the gym to keep herself fit.

"Okay. You're done."

Taylor's eyes open slowly. She stares at the girl in the mirror. It's her, but it isn't her.

"What d'you reckon?"

"I look . . ."

"Beautiful. Amazing. And at least eighteen."

"Eighteen?" Taylor feels dizzy and glowing and shining bright. She almost needs to hold on to something. She tries to pin herself back down, "Maybe not quite . . ."

Kat steps back a pace, her head on one side. "You do. With that tight jumper, and if you had some decent trousers instead of that old school skirt. And heels. You'd need heels." She sags suddenly. "I wish I had some money. I'd get you everything you need."

"Don't be nuts." Taylor is filled with a rush of warmth. "You couldn't spend your money on me."

"I would if I could." Kat's voice has gone flat. "But maybe soon—if the modelling suddenly takes off."

"Do you do modelling too?" Taylor isn't surprised. It seems obvious.

"I did lots when I was little. Catalogues and brochures and stuff like that. I was in a telly ad once. If you ever come round I'll show you the video."

Taylor pictures a miniature Kat, all blonde curls and sweet giggles. "What was it for?"

Kat pulls a face. "You won't believe me."

"I will." It's true. Taylor will believe anything.

"It was for toothpaste. I had to be this naff little kid whose tooth falls out and she sticks it under the pillow for the fairies. She's expecting fifty pence or something, but the fairy leaves a whole treasure chest full of dosh because the tooth is so white and wonderful." Kat suddenly twirls around the changing room, acting the scene, her face glowing with the memory.

Taylor giggles.

Kat comes back to the mirror. "We had cupboards full of free samples for a while. Me and Mum got sick to death of it."

"It sounds great." Taylor doesn't care what it was

that Kat advertised. If she'd told her she'd had to bounce round the garden trailing loo roll from her mouth she'd have thought it was wonderful. "Why don't you do it now?"

Kat hesitates. "I do—sort of."

"Why only sort of?"

"It's not so easy to get work when you're older. It takes money. I have to keep my hair good. My skin good. And most of all, I need the right clothes. I can't turn up to audition for photo shoots in rags. And with Mum not working at the moment . . ."

"Does she still try for modelling jobs too?"

"No." Kat's eyes darken, like a shutter coming down. "It's just—it's too hard to explain. . . ."

Taylor wishes she was the hugging sort. She wants to let Kat know that she understands. She doesn't need to know what it is that's hard for her and her mum. But she's got a stronger link with Kat than she'd realized. They've both got stuff going on at home. "It'll work out, I know it will." She touches Kat's arm.

Kat brushes her away. She seems bristly. Almost angry. "What are you—a Fairy Godmother or something?" She peels off the shirt she was trying, and lets it drop to the floor. "I'll wait for you outside." She stuffs the silky black bag back into her rucksack, and swings away out of the changing room.

Taylor battles to get back in her school shirt. She feels hot and shaky. Her fingers fumble with the buttons.

She's pressed Kat too hard—maybe made her say things she didn't want to say. She knows what that feels like. People do that to her sometimes too.

The Walkie Talkie girl comes in pushing a vacuum cleaner. "Any good?" She looks flat again now. Taylor thinks that the batteries didn't last long.

"Er—everything was a bit big." Taylor lifts down the tops she was trying on, unhooks the tokens, and picks up the shirt Kat dropped.

"It's okay. I'll take them." The Walkie Talkie girl bundles the clothes over her arm and flicks the switch on the cleaner.

The drone of its motor follows Taylor outside.

Kat is sitting on the wall by the water fountain, staring down into the scatter of gold pennies.

"Are you all right?" Taylor hovers awkwardly.

"Why shouldn't I be?" Kat shrugs. Then she glances at her watch. "But I'd better run. My mum will give me hell if I don't sort out dinner."

Kat is already moving off. Taylor falls into step beside her.

They don't saunter now. Their steps are brisk. Hurried.

The wind outside the precinct is icy. It gets inside Taylor's mouth as she breathes. It hurts her teeth and freezes her throat. She thinks about ice forming inside her lungs. With each breath she takes they will seize up a little more. Maybe they will lock solid. Maybe this will be the end of her. But she won't put the Yeti on. She won't be the person the Yeti turns her into.

Kat veers off suddenly halfway along Sandy Lane. "See you around."

"See you." Taylor watches Kat swing away into her house. It looks shabbier than Taylor had imagined, but then things are hard for Kat and her mum at the moment, and Taylor is in no position to judge.

She hurries on, taking a shortcut through the park. The path is frosted hard, glittering in the lamplight. Everywhere is quiet. Empty. But Taylor still doesn't put the Yeti on. She doesn't know who might be about to turn the corner, and she wouldn't want anybody to see.

9

Mum is watching a quiz show on the telly.

Taylor walks into the room. She is colder than packed ice. "I'm home."

Mum gives her a tired smile. "Grandad rang. He woke me up."

"Sorry." Taylor knows that she should have been around to answer it. Mum shouldn't be disturbed. But then, suddenly, she feels irritated. It's not as if she goes out that much. Not like Sam and Sophie. Mum should be able to manage something simple like answering the phone.

Mum turns back to watch the telly.

There's a bloke in a spangly white suit reading a question off a card.

Contestant Number Three—Sheila from Sheffield—is smiling. The smile reminds Taylor of a magic show she saw once. She was about six, and she went with Sam and Sophie to see a magician. He wore a big top hat and threw knives round the edge of a lady in a glittering gold swimming costume. Taylor pretended to cover her eyes, but she kept her fingers splayed open. It fascinated Taylor that the lady in the swimming costume kept smiling.

Taylor rubs at her hands. The numbness is going now, and they hurt. She wonders if Mum will notice that she's pinched blue and shivering. She wonders if Mum will say, "You must be frozen." She doesn't. Taylor thinks how easy it would be to stay properly frozen. And how painless. "What did Grandad say?"

A buzzer sounds on the telly. There is a burst of clapping. Sheila from Sheffield has won a set of beach towels.

"Betsy's fixed. He's coming Friday."

"That's good."

"I haven't done dinner yet. My head . . ."

"It's okay." Taylor cuts her off quickly. "I'll sort it." A thought spins into her head of Kat sorting dinner back in Sandy Lane. She likes the idea of it—both of them doing the same thing at the same time. It's a lot better than the thought of Sam and Sophie curled up together reading *Girl Talk,* giggling about dyeing their eyelashes green, or tattooing their foreheads with pictures of Rikki Cavalier. "I'll just take my stuff upstairs."

Mum's fingers pick absently at the fluff on her dressing gown. Her eyes are still fixed on the screen, but Taylor knows that she isn't watching. The quiz show is bouncing off her, like light hitting rock. It can't get through.

Taylor heads up to her room.

She unpacks her rucksack, taking out the lilac shimmer lipstick and the sparkly foil wrapping paper. She puts them on the dressing table amongst a collection of tiny ornaments, odd-shaped stones, and Grandad's star box.

From downstairs she hears the buzzer again. More clapping. Sheila from Sheffield has won herself a leather suitcase.

Taylor blocks out the sound. Standing back for a moment, her head on one side, she studies the effect she has just made. These are not just ornaments and odd-shaped stones. These are not just bits of foil paper and a lilac shimmer lipstick. They are personalities. They have energies. Moods. They change depending on where she puts them. And she hasn't got this quite right. The foil is in the wrong place. She slides it sideways, nearer to the star box. But then the lipstick is wrong. She needs to bring it forwards more.

From downstairs the buzzer is more frantic. The clapping wilder. Sheila from Sheffield has won the video camera. Now she is trying for the holiday in Florida.

Taylor tries pushing the star box farther back. Putting the foil at an angle. The lipstick on its side.

A hooter blows. The sound is lower. Deeper. Very

different from the buzzer. The hooter says "thumbs down." "Hard luck." "Tough." There is a bright spangle of music. The quiz show is finishing. Taylor wonders if Sheila from Sheffield will cry in the car on the way home.

The lipstick doesn't work on its side. It has to be standing up. Taylor moves everything faster, shuffling it all round, and then putting it back where it was in the first place. She has to get this right. It's her and Grandad and Kat. They all have to balance together.

She picks up Grandad's star box and holds it away from her, at arms length. She can't take her eyes off it. It's glowing. Glittering. She tilts her hand slightly. The stars catch the light. They are magical. Beautiful.

Suddenly a picture swims up through her memory. She sees a glow of twinkling silver amongst a forest of swaying reeds. She hears a child's voice singing *"Row row row your boat, gently down the stream . . ."* She tries to push the memory away, but the singing goes on and on. *"Merrily, merrily, merrily, merrily, life is but a dream . . ."* Taylor realizes her hand is trembling. Not just trembling, really shaking. The hand jerks sideways, as if it is nothing to do with her. She has no control over it. The star box falls. It rattles down onto the dressing table. Some of the sequins break off. Taylor stares down at it, feeling as if her stomach is shrinking. She has spoilt Grandad's beautiful box. She spoils everything. She isn't safe to touch things. She isn't safe to be around. She can't be trusted with anything special. Or anyone . . .

Looking up, Taylor struggles to find her face in the dressing table mirror, but her reflection is blurry, as if there is water rushing past. Her lungs ache. She has to breathe. She *has* to breathe. But if she opens her mouth the sea will flood in. And she knows it only takes two minutes . . .

From downstairs, Taylor hears the sound of someone screaming.

Taylor is jolted into the present.

She runs—almost slides—down the stairs.

The front room is shadowy. For a moment she thinks she sees rocks and weeds, and strange flashes of light.

And then she sees Mum, asleep on the sofa—it *is* only the sofa—the old beige dressing gown pulled tight around her.

Taylor leans back against the wall—it *is* only the wall—and makes herself breathe deep, slow breaths that fill her lungs and make the shaking stop.

Across the room the television—it *is* only the television—flashes out light and colour. It is a holiday programme. A party of children are being bounced behind a yellow banana boat through the sea. The spray drenches them. They are all clinging to each other. Laughing.

Screaming. Along the bottom of the screen a printed message gives details of fourteen days self-catering for four people at the Apollo Apartments. And that was it. That was all it was. A holiday programme, drifting up through the ceiling into Taylor's room. Into Taylor's head.

Taylor turns on the light. Mum opens her eyes, blinks twice, and pushes her hand wearily through her hair. "Are you all right?"

Taylor shrugs. "Why shouldn't I be?"

"I just thought . . ." Mum struggles to sit up. "Why are you leaning against that wall like that? Are you ill?"

"No." Taylor is startled. She lets the nightmare drain away. It was just a crazy five minutes. She let the monsters in. But this is a new danger. Mum has noticed something about her. In a minute she might spot the makeup. She might ask questions. And if she starts asking questions she might not stop.

Taylor doesn't want questions.

She doesn't want quizzes.

She keeps her voice deliberately sullen. "I'm just knackered. First day back at school sucks."

"Don't talk like that." Mum picks at the sleeve of her dressing gown. "If you're really too tired, maybe I should do dinner tonight?"

Taylor smiles the smile of a lady in a glittering gold swimming costume. She could step right inside the telly for this one. Contestant Number Four. Taylor from

Tillingham. "Don't worry. I've already sorted something for tonight."

In her head there is a burst of clapping and the buzzer sounds.

Sam and Sophie come bubbling down the school corridor. "Have you got your ticket for the school disco?" calls Sam.

"They went on sale this morning," adds Sophie.

Taylor stops and waits for them. They're wearing lipstick to school now. "I don't know. I'm not sure I'll be going."

"Of course you are. It's going to be wild." Sam glances at Sophie with a "she's gone completely bonkers" expression on her face.

Taylor feels a prickle of irritation. Have they forgotten she had her purse nicked? What do they think she's going to wear?

Sam and Sophie move in on either side of her, their arms linking through hers. "Are you coming to lunch?" They say this together, as if it is a line in a play that they have been rehearsing.

"I went shopping last night. Into Tillingham." Taylor

says this suddenly, ignoring their question about lunch. She wants them to know she has other things. They can't just pick her up and drop her.

Sam asks, "Did you buy anything?"

"I was just looking." Taylor waits for them to ask her who she went with.

"I went shopping last night too." Sophie gives a sudden giggle. "It was on the Internet."

"Oh—I did that as well." Sam gives an excited squeal. "I ordered these really wild sweatshirts. They're designer label and everything. They were half price."

"Have you tried that 'Shop till You Drop' Web page? I opened it up at the weekend. I stayed on it for over an hour. My dad went nuts . . ."

They are talking across Taylor now, their sentences like party streamers criss-crossing between them. They don't throw any streamers to Taylor, and she couldn't take one if they did. She doesn't know anything about designer labels. She hasn't got the Internet. She hasn't even got a computer.

Taylor slips her arms away from theirs, pretending to bend and tie her shoelace. They glance down at her, but they don't stop talking. And they don't stop walking. They are moving on, away from her, more and more streamers whizzing backwards and forwards between them, binding them closer.

"Hey. I've been looking for you."

Taylor straightens up, and turns to see Kat grinning

at her. She has a sudden fierce longing for Sam and Sophie to look around. "Hey."

"How's things?"

"Fine. I had a brilliant time yesterday." Taylor says this hurriedly, the words rushing out of her. She wants to let Kat know that, even though it went a bit flat at the end, it didn't matter. And she wants to talk about shopping. She wants Kat to start handing her party streamers.

Kat shrugs. "It sucks though really, doesn't it?"

"What does?" Taylor feels her streamer drop through her fingers. Kat hasn't even tried to catch it.

"Shopping—with no cash. I was really down about it in bed last night."

Taylor feels like a party balloon losing air slowly. For her, shopping had been the one decent thing about yesterday. She'd thought about it all the while she was stirring up meatballs and rice. She'd made a story in her head about going again. Not tonight of course— that would be too soon—but she'd pictured the week-end. Maybe Kat would come round for her. Or she'd go round for Kat. It didn't matter which. They'd saunter about. Try things on. Have a laugh.

Now Taylor feels pathetic. Perhaps yesterday wasn't that great. Perhaps she just made it up. She makes her voice casual. "I just meant it was different. It killed a bit of time."

Kat shakes her head. "I'm just sick of being broke.

Never actually buying anything. I mean, trying stuff on is great for a while, but when you get home—" Her eyes get that shuttered look again. "Well—you're back in the real world, aren't you?"

Taylor nods slowly. She wonders what else they could do together. "Do . . . do you want to meet up at the weekend anyway? We don't have to go shopping. We could go to the park."

"Boring boring boring." Kat pulls a face. "I can't be bothered."

There is a pause.

"I've got money for the housekeeping. Maybe, if I put a bit by each week . . ." Taylor trails off. She's not even sure what she's talking about.

There is another pause, and Taylor begins to wonder if Kat is even listening. Suddenly Kat kicks at the wall. "The stupid thing is, I've got dosh in my bank, but I have to wait till the end of the month to get it out. My aunt Bev sent a cheque for Christmas, to get clothes with. She always sends me money—she says she's lost touch with what I'm like now—but it's a pain. You have to wait twenty-eight days for the cheque to clear— that's not much use with the school disco in three weeks' time."

"Oh—right." Taylor doesn't know much about how cheques work.

Two boys come up and nod at Kat, passing on either side of her.

Kat flicks her hair backwards. "Look, I'll be at Supa Shoppa around ten on Saturday morning. If you come up there, we'll talk about it then. I've got to run now."

"See you." Taylor watches her race up behind the two boys, nudging and poking both of them, laughing. The boys nudge and poke her back. They all three grab hands, pulling each other, wrestling. Kat shrieks and breaks away. The boys chase after her. The three of them disappear round the corner.

Taylor tries to imagine nudging and poking boys like that. She can't quite see it. They'd probably think she was trying to attack them, and punch her on the nose. Or maybe—worse still—they wouldn't notice. Maybe they'd just carry on walking.

Sam and Sophie appear suddenly from around the corner. "Hey—where did you get to?" says Sam, linking her arm through Taylor's.

Sophie catches Taylor's arm on the other side. "You missed lunch," she says. "Lasagne and chips. They've closed the hatches now."

Taylor lets herself be guided back down the corridor between Sam and Sophie.

She has only just noticed how much her stomach is rumbling.

11

It is Friday afternoon.

Taylor walks home from school more quickly than usual.

Friday is Grandad day. It's better than all the others.

He meets Taylor at the door. "I've cooked you chicken curry," he says.

"Sounds great." Taylor hangs her rucksack on the hook in the hall and follows him into the kitchen.

"Don't say that until you've tasted it." Grandad's big warm face is all crinkly and kind. He always rustles up something from the fridge and Taylor has it on a tray in the front room.

Taylor watches him stir the sauce.

It phutters softly, as if it is gurgling to itself. Blowing bubbles.

Taylor is happy that Grandad is here. There is the smell of food that she hasn't stood in the empty kitchen to make, the radio murmuring in the background, the feeling that the heart of the house is beating again. Sometimes Taylor wishes that Grandad could live with them properly, but Mum won't let him. She heard them arguing about it once. Mum insisted they were fine. She said they would get through it on their own. Grandad must have believed her, because he went home soon after that. But that was the day Mum locked the door on Laura's bedroom and went to bed for two days. She didn't even open her eyes when Taylor tiptoed in.

Taylor leans closer to Grandad. He is so solid. A rock for her to swim to.

He smiles down at her. "I did the garden, too. I've tied back a few bushes and swept your leaves for you."

"Thanks." Having the garden done is even better than the curry on a tray for Taylor. She always copes with the house. The house doesn't fight against her. If she puts something down, it stays there. If something is grubby, or spilt, she cleans it up. It is a job finished. She can put a tick beside it.

The garden is different.

It does things on its own, when she's not looking. It spreads grass and nettles and tangles of brambles. Cobwebs stretch across the swing and the Wendy House. Ivy creeps along the fence and tries to get in through the kitchen door.

She did try, at first.

She battled with the lawn mower. She pulled up weeds. She cut back bushes until her fingers were scratched and blistered. But it was the roses that finished her. They bloomed suddenly one day, a whole shower of them, their colours golden and glorious and shouting life and triumph and the sense that the world was a wonderful place to be.

Taylor saw them through the kitchen window when she was peeling potatoes.

She grabbed a knife and ran outside. Then she cut them down quickly, fiercely, tossing their golden heads onto the ground. How could they grow like that? How *dare* they grow like that? And even then, it wasn't over. She could see more buds, some almost ready, and some just the tiniest beginnings. She hacked at them, not caring that the thorns were scratching her arms and the bare skin on her legs.

It was then that Grandad arrived.

He took her hand and led her inside. He made hot soup and toast even though it was high summer.

Since then he has come for the day every Friday—and Taylor has stayed away from the garden.

"One chicken curry—would madam like to see the sweet menu later?"

Grandad touches Taylor's shoulder and she pulls herself back into the present. She slips into the game. "I normally go for the chocolate gâteau," she smiles. "But perhaps if you've any fresh strawberries . . ."

She wouldn't do this if Sam and Sophie were here.

She especially wouldn't do it in front of Kat.

But she knows Grandad's just being kind, like someone playing "tea parties" in the Wendy House with their kid sister.

12

"What's the time?" Grandad is waking up.

Taylor is doing a sketch of his hand which is stretched along the arm of the chair. She hadn't wanted to do his face. It had looked too old in sleep—older than she wanted to think about. "It's nearly five thirty."

"Time I got off." Grandad pulls himself upright and rubs his shoulder. "Monty will be sulking otherwise. Sometimes I think I'm a slave to that cat. Your mum's got her pills—she's got some new ones to try out—and I've put this week's money on the mantelpiece. Is there anything else you need?"

"No." Taylor smudges the outline of the thumb and begins shading in round the fingertips. "I'm fine."

"I can send you extra if you need it."

"I don't."

Grandad lifts himself from the chair. "I'll just go up and check on your mum, then. See what she thought of the curry."

"Okay." Taylor doesn't go upstairs with him. She never does. She likes to wait till he's gone before she lets the real world wash in again. She stares at the hand sketch for a moment. The fingers are bent. Knobbled. Like branches. She thinks of that hand now, out in the garden, doing things with bushes and leaves that she cannot face. She labels the picture "A Helping Hand," and wishes she was better at sketching. She ought to practise more.

Grandad is back in less than ten minutes. "Mind you ring now, if there's any problem. Any problem at all."

"Okay." Taylor goes with him to the door.

She already feels the ache settling in her. It is always worse for a while, just after he's gone.

He turns to hug her. Taylor's hair rubs awkwardly against his rough stubbled chin. He smells of leather and wood and things that are safe and strong.

For a wild second Taylor wants to cling to him. Never let him go.

"Are you sure you're all right?" His eyes seem to search right into her, trying to follow the paths in her mind.

She smiles, pulling back from him. "You get going. Thanks for coming."

"Take very, *very* good care of yourself." He touches her cheek, wrestles into his thick heavy coat, and is gone.

Taylor listens to Betsy start up.

She doesn't go outside to wave. She never does.

As Betsy's grumbling rattle fades away, Taylor turns and walks back into the front room.

The house has sagged again. Taylor thinks it is like a sick person who perked themselves up for a special occasion, but now there is no need to pretend anymore.

She slouches in front of the telly.

Part of her wishes Grandad hadn't made the curry. It's better when she has to cook. It's better when she's keeping busy.

There's a chat show on—the sort where the audience cheer and boo. Tonight it's about teenage superstars. Taylor lets herself get lost in it. She wants to be one of the beautiful string-thin girls with long swishy hair. The girl at the end of the row reminds Taylor of Kat. Her mum is with her, beaming proudly, telling the audience that she doesn't care what the girl who looks like Kat does, as long as she's happy. This makes the audience happy too. They clap and cheer. The girl keeps smiling round at everyone, her eyes glistening with grateful tears. The mum takes hold of her hand and they lean together. The camera closes in on them. Taylor can see that the mum looks like the girl. Or the girl looks like the mum—whichever way round it works.

One day, Taylor is sure, the real Kat will be on a programme like this. She'll get there in the end, shining brighter than whatever crap it is she and her mum are stuck in at the moment. She hopes she still knows Kat when that happens. She wishes she could be part of Kat's rise to glory in some way. She might not be able to sort out the mess of her own life, but she could do wonderful things for Kat.

Taylor flicks the switch on the remote control, and finds another chat show. It's about people in debt. People who can't pay their bills. They look tired and worried, and Taylor doesn't want to watch them.

Her head is still buzzing with thoughts about Kat. She hasn't seen much of her all week. Only from a distance—and each time she's been with two blokes. They're always laughing. Messing around. Taylor has never felt brave enough to go over to them.

She hopes Kat turns up tomorrow.

It won't matter to Taylor what they do. It'll just be good to be with her.

Upstairs she hears the bed creak. Slow footsteps pad across the landing and down the stairs. Mum's head appears round the door. Her hair is thin strings. Her eyes are empty. The skin on her face is sludge grey.

Taylor thinks it's a good thing she has never wanted to be a model.

13

"Hey." Kat is sprawled along the bench by the post-box. She looks almost animal in a leopard-spot jacket and tight black trousers.

"Hey." Taylor is wearing her old jeans and sweat-shirt. In her back pocket is the brown envelope of money that Grandad left. She's got to get the food in later, but not yet. There's loads of time.

Kat rubs her arms with her hands. The leopard-spot jacket is flimsy and thin. Kat keeps shivering. Taylor remembers standing with Sam and Sophie—and the boring "Mum-type" comment she'd made that day she got her purse nicked. *You must be frozen.* Now she wishes she had a thin, unsuitable jacket to stand and shiver in.

"I might not stay long." Kat picks a scratch in her gold nail varnish, then stares past Taylor. She seems worlds away. "I just didn't want to let you down."

Taylor has the stupid feeling that she might be

about to cry. Kat—who must have a million things she could be doing on a Saturday morning—doesn't want to let *her* down. She wants to hang on to this. She doesn't want to let it go. "What are you going to do?"

Kat pulls a face. "It's too cold. I might just go home."

"How . . . how about going shopping? At least the precinct's warm." Taylor's mind whispers *say yes say yes say yes.*

Kat starts chipping at another fingernail. "I told you yesterday. There's no point."

"It's something to do." Taylor kicks at an empty cigarette packet by the bench and tries to make her voice echo the flatness of Kat's. But inside she is filling up with a reckless, spinning urgency. She doesn't want Kat to go home. She doesn't want to go home herself. If she can go with Kat today—if she can build up that buzzy mood they were in before—Taylor is sure they'll click together properly. Kat will see that they don't need money. They can have a laugh without it.

Kat stretches, stands up, and kicks the cigarette packet back to Taylor. "I'll just feel shitty. There'll be other kids from school there, all buying stuff. It'll just remind me of . . ." She shrugs, then meets Taylor's eyes, ". . . of everything I can't have."

And then Taylor says it. And as she says it, she realizes she's known all along—probably even since yesterday—what she is going to do. She doesn't plan to spend it all. Just half. And it's only for this week. She'll never do it again. "I've got cash," she says, pulling Grandad's brown envelope from her pocket. "I can lend you some till your bank cheque goes through. I've got a bit to spare."

"Mirror mirror on the wall, is my bum big or is it small?" Kat is twisting round in front of the mirror in the Night Life changing room, trying out a short denim skirt with metal studs all over the pocket. She is fizzy bright, almost glowing. Her eyes dance as she stares at her reflection.

"You look great." Taylor giggles and slips on a jacket that is the colour of creamy vanilla. She wonders if she'll be cold enough in it. The thought makes her giggle even more.

"What's the joke?"

"Nothing. It's too hard to explain." Taylor keeps giggling. She's been giggling since she got here. She moves closer to the mirror and pushes her lips into a pout, but the giggle stays behind the pout, as if it's running round inside her mouth.

"You look great too." Kat flicks her eyes over her. "Although you'll need makeup. It's a basic requirement.

Otherwise you'll only ever be half dressed."

Taylor studies her face. Kat's right. She looks too pale. But even without makeup she feels excited. Her old self—the old Taylor—is being pushed out of her. Or maybe it's just moving aside, making room for this new one to get in. Taylor's not quite sure who she is yet, but whoever she's turning into, it's someone she likes. It's someone who might have a fizzy bright glow and dancing eyes. It's someone who might get lifted onto the shoulders of Upper School boys and carried off down the corridor.

"I'm going to get this." Kat smooths the denim skirt down over the fronts of her legs. "I can always bring it back."

Taylor is half turning, still looking in the mirror, wondering if she should be worried about her own bum. "What d'you mean?"

"This is our first stop. We'll be trying stuff out all day. I might see something I like better somewhere else."

Taylor thinks it sounds complicated. "Why don't we just come back for it later?"

"It might be gone. It's the only one my size." Kat reaches into her bag and brings out a lipstick. She stretches her lips and colours them plummy red.

"What if they don't take it back?"

"Of course they will. It's a Refund Promise. You get twenty-eight days to make up your mind."

"But . . ." Taylor feels as if a brake has been pulled on inside her. What if they *don't* take it back? What if Kat loses the receipt? What if . . .

"What's up?" Kat stuffs her makeup back into her bag. She wriggles out of the denim skirt and slings it over her arm.

"Nothing." Taylor slips the vanilla cream jacket off and puts it back on its hanger. She feels as if she's flattening out—as if the old "yeti-wearing" Taylor is pushing her way back in. And Taylor doesn't want her back. She stares in the mirror. She wants to be different. It's good to be different. She *has* to be different. Slowly her eyes change from a rabbit in headlights to a leopard out hunting. "Come on then," she says suddenly. "If it's that easy, I'm getting this jacket, too. Let's go."

And so they go, through all sorts of shops.

Cheapo shops.

Snobby shops.

Weird tucked-away-in-the-corner shops.

Kat takes the denim skirt back and gets a black lace blouse in Razzle.

Taylor swaps the vanilla cream jacket for a silver waistcoat in Dream Baby.

Kat's black lace blouse becomes a chunky green cardigan from Girl Gang.

Taylor's waistcoat, after a nail-biting ten minutes, transforms into a slinky purple dress from Reflections.

They move through skin-tight white trousers, big baggy jumpers, and beaded silk skirts.

In Face Paints Kat finds Taylor two "gooseberry fool" eye shadows for the price of one. Raspberry blusher. Dark damson lip gloss. Honey fudge foundation mousse. The makeup takes more of the housekeeping money than Taylor thought it would, but it's still okay. She can get the Supa Shoppa baked beans instead of Heinz. They'll get by on a smaller box of tea bags.

"I think we've tried on everything in the whole world," she says at last. They are outside the photo booth in Boots, waiting for passport-size pictures of the two of them pulling stupid faces.

"And d'you know what?" says Kat.

"What?"

"I've decided I want that denim skirt I saw at the beginning."

"Oh great," says Taylor, with a mock heavy sigh. "So you mean we've done all this for nothing. We could have gone home after the first half hour."

"We could have done." Kat seems to miss the joke. Her mood changes suddenly. Her voice becomes snappy. Scratchy. "We could have spent the day shivering in the park or stuck in our rooms not knowing what the hell to do with ourselves."

The mood switch frightens Taylor. "I'm just ribbing you. It's been a brilliant day." The photos feed out from the side of the booth. She takes them out and looks at them. They're grinning. Pulling faces. Having a laugh. She wants Kat to say something funny about them, but she has turned away, staring moodily out of the shop door towards the fountain.

Taylor struggles for the right thing to say. "D'you know what?"

"What?"

"I'm doing the same as you. I'm changing this purple dress for the vanilla cream jacket."

Kat turns and stares at her for a moment, then giggles. Everything lights up on her again. "You're nuts," she says, "We both are. Let's have a look at those photos."

They lean together, their heads touching. "I look so awful."

"Well, what about me—my eyes look so *weird.*"

And Taylor knows that it's happened. They've clicked together properly.

A gang of two.

15

The radio is on in Supa Shoppa.

The music is thin and watery, like sound with the colour washed out.

Taylor picks up a wire basket and glances at herself in the security monitor.

She looks different.

She feels different.

She is alive and buzzing and full of bright colours.

She walks quickly down the aisles, the basket over one arm, the Night Life carrier bag over the other. She doesn't have a trolley. She can only buy what she can carry home.

She has a list with her, full of things like loo roll and toothpaste. She never uses this list—she remembers it exactly—but writing it down helps her hold it in her head.

She has planned the week's meals on this list.

Pork chop on Monday.

Pizza and baked potatoes Tuesday.

Ham salad for Wednesday.

This is the sort of way Mum used to shop, although she didn't do it in Supa Shoppa. Mum used to drive up to the superstore that sprang up just outside Tillingham two summers ago. Actually, it didn't spring up at all. It took ages to get built. But at the time, the local papers were filled with the horror of sinister superstores that sprang from nowhere in the dead of night.

Taylor's class did a project about it at school. Taylor made a collage. She did a huge supermarket lurking under the ground, all made out of "special offer" coupons. Just one tiny corner of the supermarket's roof was poking through the green crêpe paper grass. On top of the grass there were flowers and bushes and people walking about happily. None of these happy people noticed the poking roof of the superstore.

Taylor doesn't suppose Mum's car works anymore.

She walks up and down the aisles, first one way, and then the other. She is suddenly noticing the prices. Everything costs so much. Maybe she should have done without some of the makeup. Perhaps she could have found something cheaper than the vanilla cream jacket.

Then she peeps down into the carrier bag and sees the jacket and she thinks that it is a million times more exciting than a basket full of food. Food just gets eaten. Her jacket will last for ever and ever.

Taylor likes the idea of her jacket lasting for ever and ever. She will have it in her wardrobe when she is a really ancient granny, and show it to visitors like some people show off old photographs.

Except . . . for ever and ever is a very long time, and she has to choose something they can eat this week. The thought hits her that, if she doesn't choose something to eat for this week, she and Mum will starve horribly. She'll never even make the ancient granny bit of her life.

She begins to worry about the jacket again.

Then suddenly a picture flips into her head. It is a picture from another school project. Britain in the Blitz. Grandad helped her with the homework. He had loads of stories about rationing and coupons and powdered eggs from America. He told her how his mum—Taylor's great-grandma—managed to make money last by turning a scrag end of lamb into nourishing stew that could last them for days. Taylor isn't sure what a scrag end of lamb is. She thinks it sounds disgusting. But whatever it is, Taylor decides that she will manage too. She will be ancient great-grandma saving her family with pots full of steaming stew boiled up from a scrag end of lamb.

She begins to stride bravely between the aisles. She is doing her bit for king and country. At least, she *thinks* they had a king then. She suddenly isn't quite sure.

There are, of course, no scrag ends of lamb.

Instead she settles for cheap sausages—the sort they had at the school barbecue one summer.

Sophie spat hers out when Sam's pain of a brother told her it was full of squashed bones and diseases. He said it was riddled with worms that would squirm their way deep inside her brain.

Taylor can't find powdered eggs. She has to settle for the real thing. She gets a tin of Spam and a litre of milk. She normally buys two litres but this is the war, and she can always water it down.

Then she chooses Supa Shoppa Breakfast Cereals, which are in a plain white box so she hasn't got a clue what she is buying.

The biggest problem is Sunday dinner.

Sunday dinner is the one that Taylor makes a big effort over. She has had to learn to get it right. She made mistakes at first—chicken that was pink in the middle, soggy soft carrots, potatoes that were either too hard to eat, or that dissolved into mush.

But she's cracked it now, and it's the one meal Mum always gets up for.

Or at least it was, until Taylor's war effort started.

Taylor stares at a "Farmer Ted's Choice Chicken" display as if it is something the Germans might hide spies round the back of, and then walks away.

She stops instead under a sign that says "Manager's Best Buys."

This week's "Manager's Best Buy" is cheese.

Taylor slides back the glass door and takes out a packet.

It's dead cheap.

It's reached its "sell by" date, but that's okay. She'll use it tomorrow. It can't go off *that* quick.

She had to make Pasta Cheese Bake at school last term. It turned out okay. Mrs. Smeeton even gave her a "B+" for it. She's still got the recipe in her Food Tech book at home. Taylor thinks it's got cream in it, but she doesn't need to buy any. There's some in the fridge, left over from last week.

Taylor drops the cheese into the bottom of the basket, and heads for the pasta. Supa Shoppa does their own range of that, too. She hopes it won't go soggy when it's cooked.

She heads towards the till. There is a small queue, and she suddenly sees all the people in black and white. She realizes she always thinks of the war in black and white—like all the old films and photographs. She sees herself black and white too, a young girl out shopping for her mother, risking the bombs for that scrag end of lamb. She thinks she should probably have her hair in pigtails.

"Twenty-two seventy-five." The assistant rings through Taylor's shopping without looking up at her.

Taylor digs around in the bottom of her bag for the last precious coins. She only just has enough.

As the assistant hands her the receipt, Taylor feels a wash of relief. She's done it. She's got a vanilla cream jacket and some stuff for Kat *and* a week's shopping. She's not just doing her bit for England. Given the chance, she could save the world.

She steps outside. The door of the war-time Supa Shoppa clicks shut behind her. Taylor lets the colours buzz into her again.

She walks back home, shifting the carrier bags from one arm to another.

She thinks that, if she doesn't do Sunday dinner, Mum probably won't even realize it's Sunday.

16

Taylor is wrong.

Mum does know what day it is. She eats half the Pasta Cheese Bake, then pushes it to one side. "A strong flavour," she murmurs. "What happened to the Sunday meat?"

Taylor thinks about scrag ends of lamb and says, "They'd run out."

"Were you late getting there then?"

Taylor stirs bits of soggy pasta round her plate and doesn't answer. This is the first time Mum has said anything about yesterday. "I went into town—with a mate."

"Sam or Sophie?"

"Neither." Taylor is uncomfortable. She has grown used to silence, with just the sound of cutlery scraping against the plates. She realizes suddenly she has grown to like it. "Just another girl from school."

It's not just the shock of conversation that is making Taylor squirm. If Mum knows it's Sunday, what else does she know? Perhaps she's seen the vanilla cream jacket hanging in Taylor's wardrobe. And if she's been checking Taylor's wardrobe, perhaps her mind's been kicking in about how Taylor paid for it. Taylor is panicking. She has to be ahead of this. "I got a jacket—in the sale."

"I thought you lost your purse?"

This jolts through Taylor like an electric shock. "I found it again." Her mind sparks and splutters. Where could this lie end? *I'd left it at home all along. An old lady found it and brought it round for me. A telly detective called Inspector Whizz discovered a broken fingernail in the bottom of my shoulder bag.*

She puts down her knife and fork with a clatter.

Mum is leaning slightly towards her. "Are you going out today?"

Another jolt. *Why are you suddenly so interested?* She remembers Grandad saying Mum has new pills. Perhaps they are working. "Maybe to the park."

"Who with?"

This is too much. Mum is pushing into Taylor's head, walking around in there, peering into dark corners. "No one. I'm just going to hang about."

Mum is watching Taylor, screwing up her eyes as if she is trying to see her more clearly.

Taylor folds her arms and stares back.

Mum seems to sag suddenly, as if the sudden burst of interest has frizzled away.

Taylor imagines the interest as a scrap of brown wire on the table between them. The ends have melted, and there are scorch marks along the middle. She thinks it was a good thing it burnt out when it did. It could have burst into flames.

Mum passes her hand over her forehead, leaning back in the chair while Taylor gets up to collect the dishes. "You go on out," Mum says wearily. "Remember my Sunday paper. I'm going to lie down for a while. I'll wash up later."

"Okay." Taylor takes the dishes and carries them out into the kitchen.

She feels a wave of relief that the pills only give Mum a quick burst of energy. She is certain that the dishes are still going to be there when she gets back.

Taylor heads for the park.

She's wearing the vanilla cream jacket. She hardly notices the cold.

She's had a go at putting on makeup. She has gooseberry fool eyes and a honey fudge face. It feels sticky on her skin.

Kat is across by the climbing frame. She's wearing the denim skirt.

She's not alone—she's with one of the boys from school, but she waves when she sees Taylor and walks—saunters—over. "Hey you."

"Hey." Taylor grins awkwardly.

They walk—saunter—back to the boy.

"This is Taylor."

The boy is on a bike. He says, "Tinker, tailor, soldier, sailor," and rams the front wheel up against the climbing frame.

Kat raises her eyebrows and grabs the boy's handlebars. "You nerd." But she's laughing.

Taylor knows the rhyme. She used to do skipping games to it with Sam and Sophie in the infant school playground:

> Tinker, tailor, soldier, sailor,
> Rich man, poor man, beggar man, thief.

The Nerd pulls a packet of cigarettes from his jacket pocket.

Taylor notices that the Nerd's jacket is leather. It's probably very warm.

He nudges Kat. "Want a fag?" he says.

Kat takes one.

The Nerd doesn't offer one to Taylor. He doesn't even look at her. Taylor is glad. She'd have had to say no. She hasn't got a clue about cigarettes. She wouldn't know how to hold it. How to light it. She's only just getting the hang of chewing gum.

She suddenly wonders what Sam and Sophie are doing.

Nobody speaks. Kat and the Nerd puff away and

stare across the field. After a moment the Nerd spits and swears.

"I'm going." Kat says it suddenly, out of nowhere.

The Nerd nods. "I'll come with you." He has one of those in-between voices—half boy, half man.

Kat looks at Taylor. "How about you?"

Taylor isn't sure what Kat is asking her. Is she wanting her to join them, or is she asking if it's time for Taylor to go too?

Taylor takes the second option. She doesn't want to risk making a fool of herself. And she's not sure how she'll fit in, sauntering to who knows where with Kat and the Nerd. "I've got stuff to get. A paper for my mum." She hopes Kat will understand this, and she seems to, because she nods and smiles. "See you around."

The Nerd spits again.

Taylor turns and walks quickly out of the park, her shoulders hunched suddenly against the cold.

17

"The makeup's good. Those colours suit you." Kat has caught up with Taylor in the school corridor.

"You don't think I've got on too much of that foundation mousse?" Taylor flicks her hair back and purses her dark damson lips into a pout shape. She has been practising this in her dressing table mirror.

"You need to rub it in a bit more round the neck."

Taylor flushes beneath the honey fudge. "Does it look really stupid?"

"No—it looks great. You look years older. You probably just need to do it in a better light." Kat steps round her and rubs at Taylor's jawline with her finger. Taylor stands still, feeling like a kid having the top button of her coat done up. "I was a bit worried about the teachers. I thought they might get at me."

Kat links arms with her. "They don't give a shit. They just have to pretend to moan, because of some stupid school rule that was made before Noah built the Ark. Makeup's just part of life now."

Taylor realizes this is probably true. "I s'pose everyone's wearing it."

"Everyone who matters. And I reckon it makes teachers respect you more."

"Do you?" Taylor is surprised by this. She's always thought being good and quiet and getting on with your work was the thing teachers went for the most.

"'Course it does. It makes you look older, so you're more on their level for a start."

Taylor squares up her shoulders. She likes the idea of being level with the teachers.

Kat rattles on, "Makeup should be part of the uniform. It should go on one of those lists they send home, like the gym class kit and the type of shoes you're allowed."

Taylor glances down at her white shirt and blue-grey tie. "It would have to be grey eye shadow and blue lipstick and absolutely no sun tans."

"Blue-and-grey-striped nail varnish."

"Blue-and-grey-striped hair . . ."

The bell goes.

Taylor expects Kat to join the rush to the tutor rooms, but she doesn't.

She edges Taylor forwards and they wander—saunter—through the jostle.

Taylor suddenly gets the feeling that the bell, and the scurry of pupils, has nothing to do with them. They belong to a different set of rules. They pass the school office.

"So what about an evening after school?"

"Sure." Taylor isn't sure what Kat is asking, but whatever it is it's fine with her.

Sam and Sophie scuttle by. They glance sideways at Taylor. She wonders what they're thinking. She hopes they're stunned that she's got in with someone like Kat. She hopes they're wishing they'd stuck with her. Not that she really cares what they think.

"Will you have enough money by then?"

"What for?"

"Shopping. There's no point in us going if you're broke again."

"I . . ." Taylor is in a corner suddenly. She can't spend the housekeeping a second time. Mum is already on to her, and anyway they're running out of things properly now. War effort or not, she's going to need basic stuff like margarine and bread. "We could just look around."

Taylor feels Kat's grip on her arm slacken slightly. "You know I hate that."

"How about if we try things on, and if there's anything special we could put it by. You've got that cheque going through in a couple of weeks, and I might be able to save a bit . . ."

"There's a big problem with that." Kat's voice is suddenly flat. "My aunt Bev died at the weekend.

Apparently she had loads of debts. It doesn't look like I'm going to be able to cash it."

Taylor's mind skids to a halt. If Kat can't cash that cheque, then how is she going to pay her back for the denim skirt?

"It's bloody sad. I was really close to her too."

Taylor gets a whiplash of guilt. What a cow she is, worrying about money when Kat's aunt has died.

Kat drops Taylor's arm suddenly. "Anyway, I'd better run. The bell went ages ago. I'll see you around."

Taylor stands, watching Kat rush away down the corridor. She wishes they'd arranged something. She wishes she hadn't gone all stupid about money. They could maybe have gone hunting for cheap jewellery or something. If she bought luncheon meat instead of bacon she could probably afford that.

"What exactly are you doing?" Mr. Stewart, the Deputy Head, booms out from behind her.

"I . . . I . . ." Taylor fumbles. She blushes. She's never even *spoken* to Old Stew Pot before, let alone been boomed at by him. "I was just going."

"The bell went over five minutes ago. What do you think this is? A holiday camp?"

"No . . . I . . ."

Old Stew Pot is in front of her now, his eyes bulging behind his glasses. "And what's that on your face? The school rule is clear about wearing makeup. Who's tutor group are you in?"

"Miss . . . Miss Hadlow." Taylor stares down at her shoes.

"I suggest you go and wash the lot off, then explain to Miss Hadlow exactly why you're so late."

"Yes."

"Yes what?" The boom is a roar. Taylor doesn't know why he has to shout so loud when he is standing so near. The whole school must be listening in.

"Yes, sir."

"And see me after school. You've got a thirty-minute detention."

"Yes, sir." Taylor is scuttling away, some small pathetic sea creature that's had its rock lifted from it.

From the corner of her eye she sees Sam and Sophie standing outside the office, handing in the register.

She's not sure how long they've been there.

18

Taylor is late for the science lesson.

"You'll be working in groups, like last week." Mr. Fife, who is Scottish and has eyebrows the colour of burnt orange, doesn't even glance at her as she hovers uncertainly by the door. "We're testing for the presence of starch in leaves. Some of you should be able to get your leaves to give off a strange red glow. We talked this through last lesson, so you should have the notes in your book. I've got the leaves prepared. There's one for each group."

"You're supposed to be with us." Sam passes Taylor on the way to collect her leaf.

"I know." Taylor walks to the bench where Sophie is fiddling with the Bunsen burner, and sits down. They have already had Art. They watched a video about famous paintings. Taylor sat on her own, and worried about whether she had made the right choice in choosing the vanilla cream jacket.

"What bit do you want to do?" says Sophie.

"How do you mean?" Taylor looks up from where she has begun a doodle of a girl in a slinky dress on the back of her science book. She doesn't want to think about strange red glows. She doesn't want to think about anything that glows. And she is still worrying about the vanilla cream jacket. She is beginning to think that the slinky purple dress would have been brilliant at the disco.

"We're writing out the equipment, the aim, the prediction, and the method."

"Oh—okay—I'll do the method." Taylor shrugs. It seems like it is the furthest away.

"Beaker. Thermometer. Tripod. Gauze. Water. Leaf. And test tube," says Sam.

"And one of those holder things with iodine in it too," adds Sophie. "So—the aim is to find out what makes the leaf produce starch. What comes next, Taylor?"

Taylor is still doodling. She wishes she hadn't worn the vanilla cream jacket to the park on Sunday. She can't change it now. If she hadn't worn it, she could have got Kat to come with her when she was taking it back.

"We've got to boil the water first," says Sophie.

"Then we stick the leaf in the water." Sam shuffles her seat closer to Sophie's. "We heat the alcohol, and drop the leaf in."

"Oh, that's a point." Sophie makes a clicking noise with her tongue. "You forgot to put 'alcohol' on the equipment list. What's next, Taylor?"

Taylor wonders if perhaps there's something wrong with the vanilla cream jacket. Perhaps there's some loose stitching, or a stain at the back that she hasn't noticed. If she can find something like that, she could take it back to the shop. Although she's not sure about the purple dress anymore. The waistcoat might be better. It goes with jeans and stuff. She'd get more wear out of it. She wishes she could talk to Kat about it all.

"So now we dip the leaf back in the water again. Is anything happening yet?"

"I think we're supposed to wait for Mr. Fife to darken the room. He's just pulling the blinds down. Can you remember what he said, Taylor?"

Taylor thinks that what would have been really good would be the waistcoat *and* the purple dress. Except she could never afford both. But then maybe she *should* hang on to the vanilla cream jacket—otherwise she's only got the Yeti, and she's never ever *ever* wearing that again.

"So what exactly have you done this lesson?" Mr. Fife appears suddenly from behind her.

Taylor isn't quick enough to turn her science book over. Mr. Fife snatches at it, frowning down at the back cover. It is like a shop changing room. Taylor has filled it with long-legged girls in jackets, slinky dresses, and waistcoats.

Mr. Fife strides to the front of the room. He holds the book high and everyone falls silent.

"This," he announces, "is obviously a young lady who enjoys my company so much she wants to come back and spend extra time with me after school." Mr. Fife fixes his eyes on Taylor.

Taylor meets the stare. She watches Mr. Fife's face flush with angry red. She thinks he is better than the science experiment. She thinks he would glow in the dark.

Mr. Fife stabs his finger at one of Taylor's long-legged girls. "End of the school day," he snaps, "I want you in here, with this book, and a good explanation as to why you think you're entitled to deface school property in this way."

Taylor looks down at her hands. "I . . . I can't. I'm already seeing Mr. Stewart."

"Oh, are you indeed. Then you'd better see me at breaktime—*and* lunchtime—every day this week." He flings the book back at her and it lands, skidding sideways, back on the bench. "Now get on with your work, all of you. I'll be turning the main light off in thirty seconds."

Taylor picks up her book and turns to Sam and Sophie. "I can't remember what I'm supposed to do," she whispers.

Sam and Sophie exchange glances. "Write up the method," Sam whispers back.

Taylor picks up a pen, then turns to Sophie. "What was it again?"

19

Taylor sees the advert on Thursday evening.

She has picked up Mum's Sunday paper, and is flicking through it, but she can't really concentrate. She's thinking about Kat. Kat is slipping out of her reach, moving away before they'd even got a chance to be proper friends. The thought of it makes her feel empty. And scared. It's as if there is a huge, aching space inside her, and for a while Kat was filling it up.

She scrumples the paper angrily, about to throw it away, when suddenly a headline shouts out at her:

EARN AMAZING MONEY
IN THE COMFORT OF YOUR OWN HOME

Taylor is drawn to the idea of amazing money. It's got a fantasy feel—like money that a magician pulls from his sleeve. She reads on.

THE SWEET LIGHT OF ANGELS

These beautiful creations—each with her own name
and distinct personality—are designed as part of an
exclusive range of collectable ornaments.

The exquisite pieces will tempt the rich and
famous. They will entrance collectors of fine art. But
we at Painted Promotions want to extend their
appeal by keeping prices within the reach of those
with a more modest income.

We are looking for a team of homeworkers—talented
people with an artistic flair and a steady hand—to
work on these exciting pieces.

Each approved homeworker will receive an initial kit
of fifty unpainted angels, sufficient paints and brushes,
and a colour chart to work from.

What could be a simpler, more satisfying way to
earn money from the comfort of your own home?

Send your form in now, and paint your way to a
more colourful future.

Down one side of the advert is a picture of a tiny,
ceramic angel. She's got curling blonde hair and big, big
eyes. There is something about the angel that pulls at
Taylor. She keeps reading:

Lily brings peace and safety to soothe the pain of
troubled souls. She has a paradise garden lush with
soft-scented flowers. When someone feels lost or

afraid, Lily hears their troubles and takes them flowers in their dreams. In the morning the dream is always forgotten, but there is a faint sweet smell that lingers in the room all day. Later, just before bedtime, the dreamer finds a single white petal on the floor. They can never work out where the petal may have come from, but they do not feel lost or afraid anymore.

Taylor finds that she is gripping the paper tightly, hugging it to her chest. Images of angels with soft blonde curls and garlands of flowers fill her thoughts. Taylor likes these angels in her head. She would like to keep them there forever. But already they are drifting away. They are a dream that she cannot hold on to.

And suddenly she thinks—if the angels were painted really carefully—really beautifully—maybe they could do some good for the people that bought them. They could be like magic charms, or golden wishing coins.

And maybe these angels could even help her to help Kat. They could paint them together. Taylor's mind runs to a string of evenings. She and Kat could work in her bedroom. They'll listen to the Rikki Cavalier tape that Sam lent her. They'll drink Coke and have a laugh, and talk about how it will be when Kat really makes it as a model. But it won't just be talk. It will be the beginning of Kat's success—the angels will open the door to fame for her. And she'll get closer to Taylor, too. They'll have a friendship that will last and last. And every weekend they'll be able to go out together buying clothes and stuff, and they won't have to rely on dying aunts or borrowed housekeeping money to do it with.

There is a form to fill in and cut out.

Taylor writes in careful block letters, but smudges the signature that confirms she is over eighteen. Somehow smudging it makes the name not quite hers. A kind of written mumble.

She sticks the form inside an envelope.

From upstairs the floorboards creak.

Mum is rising again.

Taylor seals the envelope quickly, and stuffs it into her school rucksack.

By the time Mum has reached the bottom of the stairs Taylor is already on her way into the kitchen to fry the sausages. She hopes that, if she cooks them on a low heat very slowly, the worms that squirm their way into your brain will die.

2 0

Taylor goes looking for Kat at school the next morning.

She finds her in "E" block, by the drinks machine. She's locked in a tussle with the Nerd and his mate. They're all laughing, and they don't notice Taylor.

Taylor wonders how to approach them. She could stand very still, clear her throat, and wait for them to look round. But they might not. They are making a lot of noise. And anyway it feels a bit like something a teacher would do—arms folded and disapproving.

So maybe she could bounce forwards with a bright joyful laugh and some sparky comment like *"Is this a private fight, or can anyone join in?"* She pictures them grinning round at her, maybe the Nerd's mate grabbing her, pulling her into a kind of rugby scrum with the other two. She, of course, will be laughing and shrieking, just the same as Kat is now.

"Hey you." Kat sees her suddenly, and gives a half

wave. It's hard for her to wave properly because the Nerd is trying to pin her arms behind her back.

"Hey."

"Where have you been? I've missed you this week."

Taylor isn't sure what "missed you" means. It could be that Kat has longed for her, or it could be that she just hasn't caught up with her. Taylor would like it to be the first, but thinks it is more probably the second. "Detention."

"All week?"

"Breaktimes and lunchtimes with Scottie in Science, and after school with old Stew Pot." Taylor's voice has a rough edge to it that surprises her. It reminds her of when they did *Oliver Twist* at junior school. Sam was the "Artful Dodger." Sophie was Nancy. Taylor wasn't anyone in the play. Or at least—not anyone that mattered. She was an orphan with a grubby grey face, and her one line was to Oliver saying, *"Go on, just ask."*

Kat slips out of the Nerd's grip. "What did you do to get in all that trouble?"

The Nerd and his mate are watching Taylor. They seem to be noticing her properly for the first time.

Taylor shrugs, as if detentions every hour of the day and night are a way of life for her. "Just normal stuff."

The Nerd gives her an odd look, and then turns back to Kat. "Are you getting a video out this weekend?"

"Maybe. What d'you want to see?"

"That new one—*The Hand*. People ran from cinemas screaming when it first came out. Loads of them fainted. There were ambulances and everything."

"Sounds great." Kat raises her own hand slowly through the air, her fingers moving like slow tentacles.

The Nerd copies her. Then his mate joins in. The three of them begin grabbing each other's wrists and gasping, "The Hand. The Hand. Oh, save me—it's The Hand."

Taylor hovers, awkward, thinking that perhaps this is not the moment to introduce home-painted angels into the conversation. *Go on—just ask.*

"How about you?" Kat is still waving her hand about, bringing it closer to Taylor's face. "D'you want to come over?"

There is a sudden silence from the others, as if Kat has just offered to give Taylor a piece of their cake. Or one of their fingers.

Taylor wants to say "yes," but she can't. "My grandad's coming over. I just wanted to tell you something."

"What?"

"It's just—" Taylor glances at the Nerd and his mate. *Go on—just* ask. "I've found a way of earning some money."

"That's great." Kat's eyes are completely locked on to Taylor now. "What is it?"

Taylor hesitates.

The bell rings.

She gets a sick, prickly feeling. She doesn't want another week of detentions. "It's just—it's a naff idea really, but it's easy. Something we could do at home."

"Sounds good."

"But it's—" She glances at the two boys. "Not everyone could do it."

Kat jerks her head at the Nerd and his mate. "Get lost. I'll see you around." She softens the "get lost" with a nudge and a grin, and neither of them seems to mind. They shuffle off down the corridor.

Taylor still hesitates. *Go on—just ask.* "I brought this to show you. I've sent off for the pack."

Kat takes the folded newspaper cutting and reads it slowly. Then she gives a snort of laughter, "You want to paint angels?"

Taylor feels as if she has been punched in the stomach. The picture of her and Kat giggling through a string of evenings grows foggy. "I mean—" She is stumbling on her words now, struggling for a way out. "I just thought w—I could get some money from it."

"Yeah. Why not." Kat flicks Taylor the sort of smile you might give to a little sister who has run up to show you her finger painting. "I think you should go for it."

Kat is walking away. Taylor has to hurry to keep up.

They reach Kat's tutor room, and she gives Taylor a

nudge. "See you around. And good luck with that angel thing."

"I might not bother with it." Taylor keeps her voice casual. "It depends if I've got time." She turns quickly and hurries towards her own room.

Miss Hadlow raises her eyebrows. "Late again, Taylor?" she says. "I think you'd better see me at break-time."

21

"You're late. Is anything wrong?" Grandad meets Taylor in the hallway.

She shakes her head. "I just—stayed behind to help Miss Hadlow sort some stuff out." Taylor is surprised how easily the lie slips out. It is like a worm of a sentence. A thin slimy thing that has squirmed its way into her brain. It doesn't seem to be anything to do with her.

"Your mum's got tummy troubles. I warmed up a bit of pasta and cheese sauce that was in the fridge. It hasn't agreed with her."

Taylor thinks about the "Best Buy" cheese and last week's cream. She can see the sauce still in the fridge, a stretch of clingfilm across it. She imagines it moving. Small transparent bugs blob about inside it.

Mrs. Smeeton showed them live bacteria in a Food Tech video once. They were disgusting. Nobody wanted school dinners that day. "Did—did you eat any?"

"Just a bit. It smelt too good to waste."

Taylor remembers when Sam's pain of a brother sneaked into their dad's shed and drank something dangerous. He was rushed to hospital to have his stomach pumped.

Grandad touches Taylor's chin with the edge of his finger. "Don't worry so much," he said, smiling.

Taylor forces a smile back.

Grandad is already walking away into the kitchen. "Tough as old boots, my insides. And I don't reckon it was the cheese sauce that got to your mum anyway. It could be the pills. Remember she's trying some new ones. Pills can do odd things to you until your system gets used to them."

Taylor follows Grandad, watching for signs of sudden collapse. But he looks well. He's brilliant for his age.

She lets herself relax. If the blobby cheese sauce bugs were going to hit on him, they would have done it by now.

And suddenly she is glad that Kat isn't going to help her paint angels in her bedroom. Something is over between them, and she is glad too that she definitely definitely *definitely* isn't going to be whizzing about like a frantic whirlpool round the shops anymore.

She'll do the angels on her own, and put the vanilla cream jacket money back in the housekeeping.

Then it'll all be finished with.

Taylor gets the feeling that this has been a sort of

warning. A lucky escape. She got out of the water before the shark arrived.

Grandad hands her a tray. "Baked potatoes and spam for you," he smiles. "The pasta is all gone."

Taylor follows him into the front room.

She eats, while Grandad shows her his sketches of driftwood that he found on the shore last weekend.

And later, after he has rattled away home in Betsy, Taylor curls up by the telly and thinks about his sketches. She's going to start doing things like that again. She's going to collect stones and leaves and scraps of this and that, and get back on with doing all the stuff she used to do before.

The doorbell rings.

It's Kat.

"Hey there." She grins. "I came round to help you check out those angel things."

22

Taylor can't believe that Kat is in her house. She feels dizzy with it. "Do you want a drink?" she says.

"Sounds good."

Taylor goes to get the Coke, and then remembers that she didn't buy any this week. "I haven't got much. Only tea or coffee. My mum's like yours. She's not working. She's been off for a while . . ." She's burbling now. Kat will think she never has friends round. She'll probably think she's boring.

"No sweat." Kat shrugs. "Tea's fine. I'm not supposed to drink it because of the modelling—Mum says it'll stain my teeth, but once won't hurt."

Taylor thinks of Kat's kitchen. The fridge will be full of mineral water. There's salad stuff on the side. No "Bargain Buy" cheese and last week's cream—and definitely no festering blobs of shuddering cheesy food poisoning.

She flicks the switch on the kettle.

Kat watches her. "Is your mum unemployed then?"

"Not exactly." Taylor fumbles with mugs and tea bags.

Kat touches Taylor's arm lightly. "You don't have to tell me. I'm not prying."

"No—it's okay. You're not." Taylor takes a deep breath. "It's just that—she's not very well."

"Hey—that's sad."

Taylor nods, although it doesn't feel sad to her. Not in the way that Kat means. Mum being ill is more scary than sad. But for Kat to understand that, Taylor would have to tell her everything. "She's . . . she's been like it since last summer . . ."

Kat is still watching Taylor.

". . . up until then we were okay really." Taylor swallows hard. Her throat is tightening. The kettle boils. The click of the switch is a click in her mind. She can't tell Kat. She's not ready for that yet. She pours the water into the mugs with shaking hands. "The stuff about the angels is up in my room. Come up and we'll have another look at it."

They go into Taylor's bedroom.

"Hey—look at all this . . ." Kat turns slowly, looking round at the collage pictures. "Did you do them?"

"Yes." Taylor rattles the mugs on to the dressing table, wishing she'd taken down "Rainbow Fairy."

"They're great. Really different." Kat goes closer.

She spends a long time by "The Great Disappearing Act"—rabbits flying out of a magician's hat like soft white ghosts. "I like the hat being pin striped like that. And that grey silk cloak. It looks like it came from a bloke's suit."

"It did." Taylor stands next to her. "It was years ago though. Mum was going to throw it out. I rescued it from the bin liner when she wasn't looking."

Kat laughs suddenly. "I like this one about the loan shark."

Taylor feels as if a window in herself is being opened, and Kat is looking through it.

Kat moves from one collage to the next. "Shells and Spells," "Roses," "Tea Party." "You're lucky. Dead lucky—having a talent like this."

"Why?" Taylor, who hasn't felt lucky for a long time, is hungry to know what she means.

Kat glances back at Taylor. "Because no one can ever take it from you. It will keep you safe."

Taylor, who hasn't felt safe for a long time either, frowns. "Safe from what?"

Kat shrugs. "I don't know. From yourself, I s'pose."

"But you've got the modelling. Surely that's the same sort of thing?" Taylor thinks that the idea of being a model is a million times more exciting than being someone who sits in their bedroom making collages.

Kat doesn't answer for a moment, and when she does her voice is very soft—so soft Taylor can hardly hear her. "No," she says. "It's not the same sort of thing at all."

She turns suddenly and walks over to the dressing table. She looks in the mirror, tossing her head so that her hair tumbles down her back. She touches the star box and the lipstick and the silver foil paper.

Usually Taylor can't bear people touching her stuff, but with Kat it feels all right. "I keep everything. I love scraps of things. I've got a pile there." She points to a box under the bed.

Kat kneels down and pulls out the stash of magazines and leaflets, a lifetime of birthday cards, foil paper, a small bundle of pens and glue sticks. "You're so organized." She empties everything onto the bed and flops down beside it. "Look at this. 'Buy one, get one free from Domino's Pizzas.'" She grins at Taylor. "You're not going to cut that up, are you?"

"You have it." Taylor creases the edges of the pages and cuts it carefully. "I'll never use it."

"Yes you will." Kat squashes it into the pocket of her jeans. "We'll go together and pay half each."

Taylor's heart does a cartwheel flip. Kat must be planning for them to go shopping again. And she can probably run to half a pizza. It won't make much of a mark in the housekeeping.

"Lose Weight Now—Ask Us How—what a load of crap." Kat fans the pile into a circle around her. "Free trial at the health club. And—what's this?" She holds up

a small orange plastic card. It is the "Spend Spend Spend" one that came just before Christmas.

"That was Mum's . . ." Taylor hesitates. She feels as if a door is opening. This is a way in to telling Kat everything. She's ready to do it. She *wants* to do it. ". . . she sent off for it back in the summer. Back before . . ."

Kat turns the card over in her hand. "It's not signed."

"Mum's never used it. She . . . she hasn't really been out since it came."

"It covers you for one hundred quid at any participating clothes store." Kat is concentrating, reading the small print on the leaflet that comes with it. When she looks up her eyes are shining, as if she's suddenly discovered the end of a rainbow. "A hundred quid, all hidden away in this tiny bit of plastic. It's magic money— and all you have to do is sign the card."

"Sounds like a dream. Until you have to start paying it back." The moment for telling Kat everything has gone. Taylor tries to match Kat's new mood.

"It's not that bad, one hundred quid. I mean, I agree, it's not good if you haven't got regular money . . ." Kat's eyes meet Taylor's across the bed. "This angel thing," she says slowly. "How much does it pay?"

Taylor knows where Kat is heading, and she wants to say no. But she feels out of control. As if she's being dragged through the sea in a banana boat. "You have to be eighteen," she says, in a quiet voice.

"I can make you eighteen." Kat's voice is even quieter. "We'll pluck your eyebrows. Sort out your hair a bit. The rest is just clothes and makeup."

"But . . ."

Kat moves closer to Taylor. Taylor wonders if she's going to put her arm round her, but she doesn't. Instead she speaks very gently, her voice almost a lullaby, "Sometimes you just have to take a grab at a chance like this. Otherwise you're the one left behind with nothing."

Taylor thinks about Sam and Sophie. She pictures them running away from her down a long dark tunnel. They are linking arms. Not glancing back. Heading towards the light. "What if the angel idea doesn't work out?"

"We'll keep the receipts. Then if something goes wrong, we can just take it all back."

"So—we won't wear it?"

"Look—you're as hooked on getting new clothes as I am." Kat nudges Taylor, as if she is a child who is refusing to dip her toe in the sea. "This is just a way to get a load more, while the sales are still on."

"I . . ." Taylor hugs her arms to her chest. She isn't sure if she *does* like having new stuff. She just likes the fun of going. Of being with Kat. But she doesn't say this. It sounds pathetic.

Kat says softly, almost whispering, "Look—we've had a crap time, you and me. We owe ourselves this."

And it is those words that do it. It hits Taylor that she doesn't need to tell Kat about what's happened in the past. Kat understands it already—and in some way it is the same for her. Their secrets are the streamers that wrap them together. "As long as we don't wear it till we've paid back the card . . ."

Kat picks up a pen and holds it out to Taylor.

Taylor takes it—and signs.

23

"Ouch!" Taylor winces as Kat leans across her and plucks out another eyebrow hair.

"Don't be such a wimp. You should try being a model. You get pushed and pulled all over the place. Have you got any cash?"

Taylor thinks about the housekeeping on the mantelpiece downstairs. She could just borrow a fiver from it. That would get them both a McDonald's and milk shake. After all, Kat *is* lending her some high shoes, a pair of cream jeans, and a lilac top. "A bit."

The bedroom door opens.

Mum hovers in the doorway. "I heard voices," she says. "You didn't tell me you had a visitor."

Kat drops the eyebrow tweezers and starts piling Taylor's hair up onto her head.

"I didn't want to wake you." Taylor's voice is clipped and tight. Mum's tied her hair back in an effort to smarten up, but she still looks as if she has been crawling through cobwebs. She thinks about Kat's mum. Kat's mum will be an older version of Kat, but just touched with the hint of their secret tragedy, like rose petals crinkling brown at the edges. "This is Kat."

"Lovely to meet you, Kat," says Mum.

"Lovely to meet you too." Kat fixes a pin into Taylor's hair and turns to smile at Mum.

Mum smiles back at Kat.

Taylor feels a sting of anger. When Mum is sad she always feels guilty. She knows it is her fault Mum is sad, and she has learnt how to live with that. It is the right way for them both to be. But Mum being happy is wrong. And a lie. How dare Mum pretend to smile like that.

"So—what are you two up to?" Mum has stepped inside the room.

"We're just mucking about really." Kat has a mouth full of hairpins, and the easy chat of a hairdresser. "We're trying out a bit of makeup before we go into town."

"Taylor doesn't usually wear makeup." Mum touches her sagging grey face and gives a nervous laugh. "But maybe I could do with a bit."

"I'll do you later. If you want me to."

"I might take you up on that." Mum's eyes dodge round Kat, catching Taylor's in the mirror. "You'll need some money if you're going out. I can't let you borrow off your friend. Take a bit from the housekeeping."

Taylor looks away. "Thanks."

"Well—I'll let you two sort yourselves out. I'm going to have a deep hot bath before I get on."

"See you later for the makeover." Kat grins.

Taylor stares down at the "ripe cherry" varnish Kat has painted on her nails. She can't believe Mum will really have a bath. As soon as Taylor and Kat leave the house, she's sure Mum will shuffle her way back to bed and let the cobwebs wind their fine grey threads all over her again.

24

"Take some of these in for me. I'm only allowed six."
They are in Fantasy, and Kat shoves a pile of brightly
striped sports shirts at Taylor.

"How many have you got?" Taylor, who hasn't managed to find anything for herself, hurries after Kat.

"Nine, I think," says Kat. "But it's 'Buy One—Get
One for a Pound.' Try a few on. I bet they'll suit you."

"Won't you mind?" Taylor catches up with her as
they reach the changing rooms.

"Why should I?"

"They're all similar." Taylor hesitates. "We'll both
have the same stuff."

"We'll just wear them different days. I'll have to
always ring you just before we go out anywhere."

They separate out into different cubicles.

Taylor gets a buzz from the thought of Kat always
ringing her. She gets a buzz from the fact that Kat is
even thinking like that. She puts the shirts on the rail.

She tries a yellow-and-orange one first. It looks ridiculous—as if she has gone in for some fancy dress competition as a bumble bee. She switches to the next one, which is red-and-green. Some of the stitching round the collar is already snagged and hanging loose. Taylor can see why the shirts are cheap.

Her hair is coming undone, hanging untidily over her face. Taylor pushes it back up, and tries the last shirt. This one is blue-and-black—better colours than the others—but the neck is wonky. It has been sewn up wrong.

"What d'you think of this?" Kat appears suddenly, fizzing in hot-pink-and-green.

"It's great." Taylor thinks that she would never have chosen those colours, but on Kat they look brilliant. "You look like you could win the Olympics in that."

Kat pulls at the front of the shirt. "I think these are blokes' sizes really. It's a bit baggy."

"It suits you. Everything suits you." Taylor steps back, looking at herself in the mirror again, wondering if she could win the Olympics in hers. It seems unlikely. She's not even sure she'd make the team for an infant school sack race. "This is wrong on me. The neck's weird."

"You're just standing funny." Kat disappears back into her own cubicle.

Taylor stares at herself for a long time, altering her shoulders, shifting her legs, changing the angle of her neck. She didn't know she was standing funny. She wonders if she does that a lot. There might be all sorts of things her body is doing without her knowing about it.

"Are you still in that?" This time Kat looks sizzling with lemon-and-blue. "Just get it. You can choose one of the others for a pound, remember. The red one was great."

"It's got a thread loose."

Kat raises her eyes to the changing room ceiling. "Just sew it back in. They're only cheapos. Take them to the till, and I'll catch up with you there."

"Which ones are you having?"

"All of them. I know the first two fit, so the others will be fine. I'll bring them out in a sec."

Taylor pulls the blue-and-black top off again, shakes out the creases, and puts it back on the hanger. Then she carries all three tops back out of the changing room.

A sales girl with an emerald-green nose stud says, "Any good?"

"These two," says Taylor. "The yellow one was a bit bright for me." She feels the need to say this, as if it is the sort of thing the nose-stud girl might want to know.

The nose-stud girl takes the shirt and hangs it on a rail behind her.

There are other customers following Taylor out.

"Any good?"

"Any good?"

"Any good?"

Taylor stands in line for the till. The "Spend Spend Spend" card feels hot in her hand.

She wishes Kat would hurry up. She doesn't want to do this on her own.

"Just these two?" A woman in a Dracula-black dress takes the shirts from Taylor.

She rings the prices into the till.

The "Spend Spend Spend" card presses deep into Taylor's skin. She is still looking round for Kat.

"How are you going to pay?" Dracula-woman is staring at Taylor. She has narrow, reddish-brown eyes. Taylor imagines her smiling. She will have pointed yellow fangs.

"I . . . I've got a card." Taylor realizes the card has dug marks on the insides of her fingers. What if Dracula-woman asks her age? What if she goes to check with someone?

And Taylor decides that she's not going to do it. She's not going to take the risk. She and Kat will have to wait until they start earning the angel money. It won't be long. And she doesn't want these shirts anyway. She doesn't even like them. "Actually, I . . ."

She feels a nudge in the back. "Hey! Look what I've found!"

Taylor swings round. Kat is behind her, waving a yellow silk jacket at her. "This is half price. I've *got* to have it." She hands the jacket to Dracula-woman and says, ice cool, "Could you add that to the account as well, please?"

Taylor feels like a mouse huddled in a corner. "What about your shirts?"

Kat wrinkles her nose. "They weren't quite right. Not for me, anyway. But yours looked good on you."

"I'm not sure that . . ."

Dracula-woman is watching them both, her reddish-brown eyes flickering from one to the other. "Is this everything?"

"I—"

"Yes," Kat cuts in. "Everything for now, anyway."

Dracula-woman swipes the "Spend Spend Spend" card through the machine. She folds the yellow silk jacket, and the shirts Taylor doesn't even like, into a carrier bag. Then she looks up and smiles.

She has beautiful teeth.

25

They move on to Glitzie's.

Kat is a whirlwind now, in and out of changing rooms, blowing about with skirts and jumpers and jackets and skirts.

Taylor is wondering what it is like in prison.

"Try something else on." Kat swirls past her. She has already put by a red chiffon dress, and is going for a black sequinned top with a hair clip to match.

"I can't see anything I like."

Kat rattles the black sequinned top back onto the rail. She does the looking up at the ceiling thing again. "I didn't think you'd be like this," she says.

"Like what?" Taylor can feel—almost see—clouds gathering between them.

"Well—I thought you'd be different."

I am different, Taylor thinks. *That's why you liked me.* "In what way?"

"More of a laugh, I s'pose."

Taylor feels rained out by this. She has failed a test. She hasn't been a laugh.

"We can go home if you want." Kat drums her fingers on the rail.

"It's just . . ." Suddenly, out of the corner of her eye, Taylor sees something she recognizes. Spiky hair—two sea anemones—standing by the checkout at the other end of the shop. They are leaning towards the stick-thin girl at the till, paying for something. Suddenly Sam looks round and stares straight at Taylor. She nudges Sophie, who turns and stares too. There is an endless moment while neither of them moves. Neither of them even smiles. They seem awkward about seeing her. Embarrassed. Then some kind of spell seems to break in Sam, and she lifts up her hand to wave. But it is too late for Taylor. If they've got such a problem bumping into her just because they meet her out shopping, then they can forget it. She doesn't need friends like that.

And she is sorry, really sorry, that she's been difficult with Kat. She knows more about Kat than almost anyone else, and she's a proper mate. Taylor's supposed to be helping her—not acting like some grumpy old aunt who just wants to get home and have a cup of tea.

She straightens her shoulders, turning back to Kat. "I'm sorry," she smiles. The smile is dazzling. Summer bright. "You're right. I'm being a drip. Let's see what you're trying on next."

26

"How come you're not wearing your new stuff?" Kat saunters over as Taylor rounds the corner in the park.

Taylor shivers in the vanilla cream jacket and realizes Kat is dressed in a "leather look" skirt and top that she got yesterday. "I—we agreed not to."

Kat nudges her playfully. "Don't *worry* so much. I've kept the labels on. We can still take it back."

Taylor forces a smile. "Yeah. Sure." She is forgetting to be a laugh again. And she has to remember that she's trying to help Kat—not be a rock round her neck. She pushes her hands into the pockets of her jacket and tries not to think about gloves.

They head for the climbing frame. The Nerd is there. He is smoking.

A picture of lungs appears suddenly in Taylor's mind. The lungs in Taylor's mind are coloured purple, the same as the lungs in the "Beautiful Body" poster on the science-room wall. They look like sea sponges. She thinks about windpipes, too. Windpipes are filled with thousands of hairs. In the magnified diagram these look like underwater plants, all soft and swaying, with the eerie beauty of things that grow deep, deep down at the bottom of the sea. It is hard to imagine all this going on inside the Nerd.

The Nerd coughs and offers a cigarette to Kat.

Kat and the Nerd start walking, as if there has been some invisible signal that Taylor hasn't noticed.

There are cracks in the paving, and Taylor remembers long ago games with Sam and Sophie. They used to play one where they mustn't tread on the cracks. Treading on the cracks would mean something bad. Taylor was never sure what the bad thing would be. Probably being told to tidy their rooms, or no videos for a week. Today she keeps her steps level, in time with Kat and the Nerd. If a crack gets in the way, she treads on it.

"Fag?"

Taylor realizes Kat is talking to her, holding out a packet with the lid open.

She flushes. Her mouth wants to say "no," but her hand is already pulling itself out from the pocket of the vanilla cream jacket. Her fingers touch the toffee-gold tip of one of the cigarettes. Kat shakes the box slightly, and the chosen cigarette slides out of the packet. Carefully, casually, Taylor holds it to her lips.

Kat leans towards her, flicking out a tiny flame from a slim gold lighter. Nothing happens.

"You have to breathe in. Inhale," says Kat.

The Nerd laughs suddenly, a short blast of sound.

Taylor is choked with embarrassment. "I know." She makes herself giggle. "I'm just mucking about."

Kat flicks the lighter again, and this time Taylor breathes deeply. A rush of smoke fills her mouth. It thickens in her throat. She feels dizzy. Sick. She wants to cough but she won't won't *won't* let herself.

Suddenly she hears a shout. "Taylor—Taylor!!"

The cough escapes, raw and harsh and angry. She looks round, still spluttering.

Sam and Sophie are chasing towards her. Taylor hates the way they are running and waving their arms about. It makes them look childish. Stupid.

"They're like a couple of bloody loo brushes." The Nerd does his belching laugh again.

Kat laughs too.

Taylor rolls the cigarette between her two fingers and lifts it to her mouth again. She takes a smaller breath. Just a tiny puff. She blows out a soft grey cloud. This time she doesn't cough.

"Taylor—" Sam and Sophie are up close now. "Your mum wants you."

Taylor's heart sinks down into the cracks in the

paving. This is all she needs—being summoned home like a six-year-old.

"How do you know?"

"She rang me." Sam stands, breathing hard. "We came to look for you."

"What did she want?" Taylor looks at them coolly, the cigarette held lightly between two fingers, the way she's seen Kat do it.

"It's your grandad." Sophie is panting too.

"What's happened?" Taylor forgets about the cigarette. Flecks of ash crumble from the tip, dusting the vanilla cream jacket.

"He's not well—"

"Your mum says it's really bad . . ."

Taylor turns to Kat. "I—I've got to go."

"Sure." Kat nods and takes the cigarette back off her. She drops it onto the path, scrunching it with the heel of her shoe. It squashes down like a dead thing.

"See you later." Taylor is walking when she leaves, but as soon as she turns the corner she is running. She jumps all the cracks in the path without even knowing she is doing it.

Mum is up. She's not dressed, but her hair is brushed.

And she's wearing a pair of blue shell earrings that Taylor made her the Christmas before last.

Taylor notices, but she doesn't comment. Not long ago she might have wished for this, but now she doesn't care. "What happened?"

"Mrs. Parker rang. You know—that nosy neighbour Grandad's always grumbling about. She said his curtains were drawn all day yesterday, and he wouldn't answer the door."

Taylor's chest tightens. She feels sick.

Mum rubs at a stain on her beige dressing gown. It is an old stain, but she frowns as if she is seeing it for the first time. She looks back up at Taylor. "I told her where to find the spare key. She went in and found him hunched up in bed. He was in a bad way."

"Sam said it was a tummy bug."

"Mrs. Parker is muttering about food poisoning. I've spoken to the doctor on the phone. He's taken samples, but it's too early to say."

"So—is he in hospital?" Taylor thinks about the blobby cheese sauce. All this is her fault. Once again, it's her fault. . . .

"He wouldn't go. You know what he's like. Says he can't leave Monty. Mrs. Parker is looking after him."

"Do . . . do you think he'll be all right?"

"He's an old man, sweetheart. Bugs and things get harder to fight as people get older."

Taylor notices the word "sweetheart," but now she doesn't care. "I want to go and see him."

"We can't do anything at the moment. The doctor's going to ring me later."

"I didn't say *we*. You don't have to come."

"He's in good hands."

"There's nothing good about Mrs. Parker's hands. She'll drive him nuts if she's faffing round him all the time." Taylor wonders what time the trains go. If there's not a train she'll get a bus. Or hitch a lift. Or run.

Mum watches Taylor for a moment, then sighs. "You can't go. The doctor doesn't advise it."

"Why not? Surely he needs proper family round him if he's really sick."

"Apparently Grandad's—well—being difficult. He doesn't want anyone there, and the doctor thinks if we force it he'll just get agitated. It won't help."

Taylor doesn't believe her. "Grandad's never diffi-cult. He doesn't get agitated."

Mum rubs at the stain again. "Sick people don't always want anyone to see them being less than per-fect. I . . . I know how that feels."

Taylor doesn't answer.

Mum pulls a tissue from her pocket and rubs harder at the stain. Then she looks hard at Taylor. "For a long time—after Laura—everything seemed too hard. I couldn't face anything, or anyone." Mum puts her hand out to touch Taylor's shoulder.

Taylor flinches away.

Mum drops her hand. Her voice is soft. Almost pleading. "I'm going to be different now. I've got new pills and I've been starting to feel a lot better. You must have noticed that. I'm going to really try."

Taylor stares down at the floor. She wants to shout that everything has seemed too hard for her, too. She wants to shout that nobody's been giving *her* tablets to help her feel a lot better. But she doesn't shout these things, because however angry she gets with Mum, there is always another voice whispering that what happened to Laura was her fault. Her fault. Her fault. And there are things that Mum doesn't know.

28

Sam and Sophie come and find Taylor at school.

They link arms on either side of her and steer her along the corridor.

"How's your grandad?" says Sam.

"Still rough."

Sam and Sophie squeeze her with their fingers. Taylor notices that they both squeeze at the same time, although they can't know that the other one is doing it too.

"Hey—Taylor . . . !"

Taylor feels a nudge in the back. Kat is grinning at her. The Nerd is hovering close behind. "Are you coming into Tillingham this week? I thought maybe tomorrow . . ."

"I'm not sure . . ." Taylor's mind is still hooked up with Grandad. "I'll have to let you know."

"I need to take some stuff back. That skirt I got is too tight." She flicks her hair, which is loose today, and shimmering with soft crimped curls. "And I need to talk to you now—about something else."

"Oh. Right." Taylor glances uncertainly at Sam and Sophie. She hasn't forgotten the way they were with her in Glitzie's, but they did do a massive search for her to tell her about Grandad. And they do seem to care now.

"Walk with us." Kat sounds more insistent. She turns to the Nerd and winks. "We've got a secret to tell you."

The Nerd's neck flushes a rich, raspberry pink. Taylor stares at it for a moment, fascinated. She has never seen a neck do that before. He nods at Taylor, his eyes not meeting hers, and rushes off mumbling something about putting the chairs out for assembly.

Sam and Sophie drop their hold on her arm. They walk away, moving on down the corridor.

Taylor calls after them, "See you both later . . ."

They don't answer. They are already turning the corner.

Kat takes Taylor's arm instead. "He hasn't really got to do the chairs. . . ." She is whispering, her voice full of hidden possibilities.

"What then?"

"He told me to tell you he fancies you."

Taylor has never had anyone fancy her before. Even right back to infant days, when Sam and Sophie were going gooey over Valentine cards and love letters with pink hearts drawn round the edges, Taylor never got any. She was stringy and gangly and she didn't expect it. "Why?" she stammers at last.

"Why not?" Kat laughs, as if this is all part of some great adventure. "He's been asking me about you. Where you live. What you're like. He's going to ask you to the school disco."

Taylor can't imagine the Nerd saying that many things in one go. "What did you tell him?"

"Not much." Kat drops her voice. "It's best to stay mysterious. You have to be a creature unlike any other. Then blokes go wild about you."

Taylor feels a flush start in her own neck. It's stupid, because she doesn't fancy the Nerd back. But she likes him fancying her. And she likes the thought of being a mysterious creature unlike any other. She thinks of next weekend, a scene where she is hanging out at the park. She is wearing a long floating dress made of soft green silk. A veil covers half her face. There is eastern music playing somewhere in the background. The Nerd appears—although somehow he is not *quite* the Nerd. He is taller. Darker. He looks more like the Rikki Cavalier poster that Sam has on her bedroom wall. The Nerd who is crossed with Rikki Cavalier leans nonchalantly against the climbing frame. Taylor twists and twirls in front of him, her fingers swaying like exotic sea plants as she moves.

"So—what shall I tell him?" Kat squeezes her arm. "I could get him to come with us tomorrow if you like.

We've still got a bit left on that card. He can wait by the fountain while we try stuff on."

The mention of Tuesday brings Taylor whirling back into the school corridor. "I . . . I said I didn't know about tomorrow. My grandad . . ."

The school bell cuts across her explanation.

Kat sighs and drops Taylor's arm. "I'll see you around then. I guess I can always go on my own." She says it with an edge to her voice, as if Taylor is a hopeless case who can't ever be relied on.

Taylor stands and watches Kat walk away.

The Nerd appears suddenly, as if he has been waiting for Kat. Taylor sees his neck do the raspberry pink flushing thing again.

Then they both disappear round the corner together.

29

The first lesson after registration is Art.

Miss Lovejoy, who has soft, white hands and long, pale fingers, has collected a great basket full of "outside things." There are twigs and leaves and clods of brown earth. "Today we are studying patterns and colours. The way things in nature balance, and the ways we can use that in our work."

Miss Lovejoy speaks in a sickly sweet voice that annoys Taylor. She stares out across the school field. The sky is darkening to a bruised grey. She thinks about Grandad, who knows everything in the world about patterns and colours.

"One of the things we need to be aware of is the subtlety of colour. See how muted this brown is? And the greens on these leaves? If we were painting these, how many shades might we need?"

Taylor picks at an edge of nail varnish left over from the weekend. She'd got most of it off with paint thinner from one of her art sets, but there are still a few patchy edges. Grandad would know the answer to Miss Lovejoy's question. He would have known the answer when he was six. He was probably born knowing. The thought comes to Taylor that he will die knowing it too.

She tries to push the thought away, but it grows bigger. She sees Grandad lying on the muted brown earth, bits of twigs and leaves with a hundred subtle shades are drifting down onto him. He is disappearing into their colours.

Taylor digs her nail into a rough bubble of skin on the tip of her thumb. She scratches at it, roughening it even more. She supposes that it hurts, but she doesn't feel it.

She is not sitting with Sam and Sophie. They are on the other side of the room with two boys who keep making them giggle. Miss Lovejoy has already spoken to them sharply, twice. Taylor wonders, without any emotion coming with the thought, whether she will ever sit with Sam and Sophie again.

Outside it has begun to snow. The idea of the snow runs round the room like a naughty child.

"I bet it's going to lie."

"They'll have to close the school down."

"We'll get sent home."

The group squirm in their seats and crane their heads towards the window.

Taylor doesn't join in with any of this. She watches

the snow coming down in whispers of white. It is lying over all the twigs, and the subtle shaded leaves, and the muted brown earth.

The world underneath will become a secret.

"It won't last." Miss Lovejoy's voice seems to come from a great distance away. "It's already raining. It'll be slush by tomorrow."

There are groans of despair. The art room is filled with six-year-olds who thought they were going to Disneyland, but have ended up with a day in the park instead.

Miss Lovejoy is coming round, handing out the twigs and leaves and clods of earth.

Taylor's finger has begun to bleed.

"Are you all right, Taylor?" Miss Lovejoy is standing behind her. Her voice is warm, and the warmth of it seeps into Taylor.

"Why shouldn't I be?" She tries to freeze Miss Lovejoy with her answer, but it doesn't work. Underneath the hard frozen layer of Taylor there is a secret pain that burns so fiercely it would blast its way through an entire ice age of snow.

30

There is a burglar downstairs.

Taylor can hear him walking about.

She lies awake, listening.

She has often wondered what she would do if she met a burglar. She's always imagined she would be bold and heroic. She'd shout and throw things and chase him away down the street. Other people would watch from behind the safety of their curtains. And when it's over they would appear outside in their slippers, shaking her hand and waiting for the police to turn up.

But this bold and heroic scene has always relied on Taylor being dressed, and downstairs. Now that she thinks about it, she realizes there is always a convenient heavy object, like a vase or a rolling pin, nearby.

This burglar who slinks into the house with the wintry dawn—while Taylor is in her nightie—doesn't quite fit the scene.

She wonders about stretching down and poking

around for her scissors under the bed, but she's not sure where they are.

She doesn't want the bed to creak.

She doesn't want to take her eyes off the door handle.

There are footsteps on the stairs.

They are coming towards her room.

Nearer.

And nearer.

"What on Earth is this?" The door swings open and Mum bursts through. She has a large cardboard box in her arms.

Taylor jerks upright. Mum looks fizzed up and wild. More scary than a burglar. "What do you mean?"

Mum drops the box on the bed. The top is torn open, brown sticky tape hanging untidily down from the lid. "The postman just brought it." Mum's voice rises angrily. "It was Recorded Delivery. The package was damaged, and I had to check the contents before I signed."

Mum pushes her hand into the box, bringing out a wad of pale pink bubble wrap. There is something grey in amongst the bubble wrap. It is a ceramic angel. It is lumpier than Taylor expected it to be, and its face has a cheap, cartoony look about it.

"It's—" Taylor feels as if a giant wave is coming for her and she can't run fast enough to escape. "I thought it would be something to do."

"There's masses of them." Mum dives her hands in

again. She brings out another one. "Some of them are broken."

Taylor recognizes "Lily," although the head is missing. She feels shaky. "I'm supposed to be painting them. They'll earn me money."

"It would take you years to get through this lot, and who do you think would buy them?"

Taylor thinks about the advert. The rich and famous. Collectors of fine art. "All sorts of people," she mumbles.

"I don't know anyone who'd buy these. You wouldn't want to win these at a fair."

Taylor feels a slow, sullen anger spreading out from somewhere deep inside her. What the hell is Mum doing getting up to answer the door for, anyway? Why is she so lively? She's got used to the old, shuffling-about Mum. She's got used to not having to answer questions. Why do the pills have to start working now? "I'll do them in my bedroom. You don't have to know anything about it."

Mum waves a bit of paper at Taylor. "I'll have to know something about them," she flashes back. "I have to pay for them for a start."

"No, you don't. You don't understand how it works. *They* pay you."

"It's you who doesn't understand, Taylor. You didn't read the small print. It's a con."

"What d'you mean?"

"You have to buy these. There's a bill here for seventy-five pounds."

"But—"

"And then, once we've paid for them, we have bought the right to paint them and sell them. To our family. To our friends. To any mug who's crazy enough to buy them."

"I—" Taylor presses her knuckles against her cheeks. "I thought . . ."

Mum puts the headless Lily back in the box and squashes the pale pink bubble wrap back down on top of it. She stares into the box for a moment, and shakes her head. When she speaks her voice has flattened again. "Seventy-five pounds is a hell of a lot of money at the moment."

"What if we just send them back? We'll say they were broken. It's true anyway."

"Except there's a bit in the small print here that says they will replace anything that is damaged. So they'll just send us more. And if I don't pay we can end up on all sorts of black lists. I may be blocked from getting credit in the future. We'll have a whole lifetime of headless angels arriving on the doorstep, and angry letters and threats from debt collectors and . . . !" Mum lets the sentence trail away, hunching forwards and staring past Taylor into some dark terrible future that Taylor can only just begin to guess at.

Taylor feels sick. She's not thinking about angels

now. She's thinking about one hundred pounds, and the "Spend Spend Spend" card.

Mum sighs, shakes her head, then straightens up slowly. "We'll sort it out later. Maybe I'll send them back with a letter explaining the circumstances. We've got bigger things to worry about at the moment. I've been awake all night, thinking about Grandad. I have to go and ring Mrs. Parker."

She goes back out through the door.

Taylor waits, listening to her footsteps fading away.

Then she scrambles out of bed.

She kneels by the box, rustling through the pale pink bubble wrap, picking out the cartoony-faced angels and staring at them. The cartoony-faced angels stare back at her with blind blank eyes. There is a colour chart in the box, and a set of paints that look like the sort a small child would have. But it doesn't matter. Taylor can't imagine that colour is going to make a lot of difference. She can't imagine how she could have ever thought that they looked like angels. She squashes everything back in amongst the bubble wrap, and pushes the lid down.

From downstairs she hears the ting of the telephone.

She pulls on her dressing gown, and hovers outside her bedroom.

"This is terrible," Mum is saying. "I can't believe . . ."

"What's happened?" Taylor races to the bottom, suddenly frantic.

"Don't worry." Mum mouths this, her mouth opening and shutting very wide, like a fish. "He's all right. Just stubborn as a mule . . ."

Taylor slips back up to her room again. As long as he's all right at the moment. She'll sort this angel stuff out with Kat, and then she'll go and see him. She doesn't care what Mum says, or even what Grandad says he wants. She dresses quickly. She notices that the white sleeve of her shirt has a smear of muted brown paint on the cuff, but there isn't time to rinse it out.

She runs back downstairs.

Mum is still on the phone. "I still can't understand what he's thinking of . . ." Taylor gets a sudden vision of Grandad refusing treatment. Mrs. Parker is trying to force-feed him with some foul-tasting medicine. The doctor is wiring him up to a bleeping machine. Grandad is struggling and a nurse with a sickly sweet voice and long pale fingers is saying, "There, there now. Don't worry, you're in safe hands."

Taylor's heart aches for him. *I'll be with you tomorrow. I'll be with you tomorrow.* She thinks these words over and over, as if somehow the invisible message can slip out from her heart, down through the telephone wires, and into his house.

Mum glances round at Taylor and covers the mouthpiece with her hand. "I'll do breakfast in a minute."

"I'm not hungry."

"You always have breakfast. And you can't go out without eating. It's not good for you."

Taylor feels the sullen grey anger flood through her again. She wants to say more. She wants to say, *How the hell do you know what I always do? How the hell do you know what's good for me?* But she doesn't say these things, because behind the anger there is still the knowledge that Mum lost touch for a reason. Mum lost touch because of something Taylor did. It doesn't matter how much better the pills can make Mum feel. Taylor has done something she can never ever, ever put right. She mutters, "I've got to go. I'm putting the chairs out for assembly this morning."

It has rained in the night and the snow is almost gone. A few snowmen slouch miserably on slushy front lawns. Taylor wonders how many colours Miss Lovejoy would find in slush.

There is a girl on the front doorstep of Kat's house, taking in a handful of brown envelopes from the postman.

She's taller than Kat, but Taylor is struck by the blonde tumble of hair. The small framed figure. The slinky oriental silk dressing gown.

She wonders if this is Kat's sister, although she hadn't realized she had one. It strikes her there are lots of things she and Kat don't know about each other. There is a lifetime of everyday things to catch up on. "I'm looking for . . ." She steps sideways as the postman turns and walks back down the path to his bike.

Kat's sister looks up from where she is staring

blankly at the brown envelopes in her hand.

Taylor feels as if she has been smacked in the face by a snowball.

The girl looking back at her is not a girl at all. It is a woman. She's got Kat's hair and Kat's build, but her face—her face . . .

Her face is bloated and blotchy. There are threads of veins that run like thin red worms beneath the yellow surface. Her mouth is tight and sour—like someone sucking lemons. It is only her eyes, puffed up and bloodshot, that hold a touch of Kat behind their bulging stare. Taylor knows, from the darkness of these eyes, that this is Kat's mother. But above the willow-slim body she seems half toad, half devil. A creature unlike any other.

"Who the hell are you?" Kat's mum's eyes struggle to focus on Taylor's face.

"I'm—I'm a friend of Kat's."

"What the hell do you want?"

"I have to see her. It's about . . . some homework."

Kat's mum gives a croaking laugh. She has yellow teeth. Taylor thinks that she hasn't made good use of those free samples of toothpaste.

"You'd better come in. The lazy cow's still in bed." Kat's mum steps backwards, motioning with her head for Taylor to follow. She stuffs the brown envelopes on a cluttered shelf by a glass of red wine. The red wine is swimming with ash and cigarette butts. Taylor notices that Kat's mum has chipped, dirty fingernails. She is glad she never got her belly pierced.

The house smells strange, of smoke and beer and something worse.

A sharp-faced man in a stained green T-shirt slams out from the kitchen, looks at Taylor, then turns and slams away again. Taylor takes in his yellow hooded eyes and snake tattoos up both arms. Taylor imagines doing a collage of this man. She would give him his normal body—and an insect's face. She would call the picture "Creepy Crawly."

Taylor thinks how wrong she was about Kat's world. She tries to remember the sad but beautiful woman that she'd conjured up in her imagination, but she can't get her back. Taylor is shocked that she could have got it so wrong. She remembers her hidden superstore, with just a tiny corner of the truth poking out through the crêpe-paper grass. "I . . . I can come back later if it's a problem," she stammers.

"It's no problem." Kat's mum squints round at Taylor, blowing smoke into her face. Then, tilting her head backwards slightly, she croaks out, "Katriona. Katriona! Get your arse out of bed. You've got a visitor."

There is no answer.

A small boy with a snotty nose and no pyjama bottoms appears at the top of the stairs and blinks at Taylor.

"She's useless." Kat's mum flicks more ash into

the wineglass. "Go on up and give her a shake."

"I don't think . . ." Taylor can't imagine herself knocking on Kat's bedroom door. She won't even know what door to knock on.

"It's first on the left," says Kat's mum. She sways suddenly, making a grab at the shelf to steady herself. The wineglass topples and the red ashy wine spills out across the brown envelopes and drips onto the floor. "Shit."

Creepy Crawly comes back out from the kitchen, glares at Kat's mum with his strange yellow eyes, and hisses, "For God's sake."

The boy with no pyjama bottoms starts to cry.

32

"Get lost." Kat's voice is thin and irritable from the other side of the door.

"It's me. Taylor."

"Who?"

"Taylor."

Taylor hears a rustle and a thud. She hears the clatter of something being knocked. The door swings open. Kat is barefoot in a crumpled silk nightgown. "What the hell are you doing here?"

"I'm sorry." Taylor is relieved that Kat is still beautiful. She looks tumbled and sleepy, but nothing has been taken away. "Something's gone wrong. I had to get you before school."

Kat pushes her hands through her hair. "You'd better come in." She steps backwards, motioning with her head for Taylor to follow.

Taylor takes two steps—and then stops.

Downstairs was one thing.

Kat's mum.

The mess.

The smell.

But this bedroom—this is something else. Taylor can't take it in. "All these clothes," she whispers.

Kat has gone to her dressing table and is pulling a comb through her hair. "I have to look good all the time. Sometimes agents hang around in shops, or parks, just looking for the right girl. I can't risk missing a chance like that."

"But there's loads . . ." Taylor stares round at it all.

A long metal rail—like the sort they have in shops—stretches the full length of the room. It is choked with trousers and skirts and jackets and shirts all crammed untidily together. There's more on the top, draped over carelessly. Taylor makes out at least three pairs of jeans. A dusky pink cardigan. A lilac silk dress hanging upside down, its long slender sleeves stretching to the floor. The dress looks as if it's reaching out, trying to stop itself from falling.

More tops and jumpers spill out of half-closed drawers. Taylor picks her way over a scatter of shoes and underwear. "You must be worth a fortune in clothes."

"I just find ways of getting it cheap. If I make it to the top, it'll pay for itself in the end. But till I get there—I have to do whatever I can."

Taylor stops by three strapless dresses hanging on

the open door of the wardrobe. There are more clothes inside, most of them just jammed in. There isn't room for anything to be properly hung. Taylor thinks that it would take at least a hundred years to wear it all. Either that, or Kat would have to get changed about every ten minutes. "I can't imagine having this much. How can you even remember what you've got?"

Kat flicks the comb against the mirror and tightens her lips. She turns to Taylor. "This is what I do, okay? This is how I have to be."

"I just—" Taylor flushes. She remembers how Kat was in her bedroom. She said nice things—wonderful things—about the collages. It's not up to her to judge Kat badly now. "I'm sorry. It's just so different to my room."

Kat watches Taylor warily. "Well, we *are* different, you and me," she says.

Taylor wants to argue that she's wrong. That they have loads of things in common. And seeing Kat's mum in such a mess has made her more sure of that. But it doesn't seem quite the right thing to say. Kat probably won't understand what she means.

Kat breaks into her thoughts. "Why are you here?"

Taylor wishes she didn't have to tell Kat. It seems to her Kat has enough to worry about. But she has no choice. "It's my mum. She's found out about the angels."

Kat rummages through a tangle of tights and tops on the floor beside her, pulls out a lipstick, and turns back to the mirror. She begins to spread the plummy red across her mouth. "So?"

"She says they're rubbish. They won't earn us any money, and I didn't read the small print properly."

"So you were ripped off?"

"I s'pose so."

"Just don't do them then. Send them back. Get your mum to say it was a mistake."

"But we needed them—to earn enough money to pay that card back."

Kat sucks in her lips, studies her reflection for a moment, then unearths a mascara from the same muddle of clothes. "So we take the stuff back. It's what we agreed. No problem."

Taylor feels a wash of relief. The angels might not be like real angels, but Kat is. She wishes she could have Kat's attitude. Laid back. Easy going. Sorting things out as they come up. "Shall I find it now?" She glances round the room, realizing that she hasn't seen any of the stuff Kat bought on Saturday. "I can take it with me. I've got my own stuff in my bag."

"You're not taking it to school?" Kat shoots Taylor a look as if she has suggested they dress up as snowmen and go and ski down the sports hall roof. "You'll get it nicked."

"Mine doesn't take up much room, but I'll get yours

after school then," says Taylor. "We can come back here and pick it up. I . . . I do have to get it sorted. I've got a problem with my grandad as well. He's really ill and . . ."

Kat begins to brush blusher across her cheeks. "I'll meet you after last lesson."

"By the gate?" Taylor still can't do the laid-back bit. She has to make this definite. "Do you promise?"

"With all my heart," says Kat.

33

After school Taylor waits by the gate.

She paces about and hugs her arms to her chest, trying to keep warm. It doesn't work. The cold bites into her bones. She wonders if noses fall off with frostbite.

She thinks about Grandad, and taking the stuff back, and what's going to happen with the angels.

She wishes she could think about something nice—just one tiny slither of a thing would do. But there's nothing nice in her head. She wonders suddenly whether, if something nice did show up, she would even notice it.

"Are you walking with us?" Sam and Sophie appear, swinging their rucksacks on their arms.

"I'm meeting Kat." Taylor glances at them, then looks away. They seem bright and fresh and happy and young. Taylor is a hundred and one. Maybe older. For a moment they all stand together awkwardly.

"See you then," says Sam suddenly. She squeezes Taylor's arm.

"And take care." Sophie squeezes the other arm.

Then they are both gone, ambling away down the road. For a long time Taylor can still hear their voices. Their chatter. Their sudden giggles.

The sky darkens and an icy sleet stings her face.

Kat doesn't come.

34

"She's out." Creepy Crawly answers the door.

Taylor's mind whirls. *She promised. She promised.* "Do you know when she's coming back?"

"No." Creepy Crawly slides his eyes up and down Taylor. "Ever had your picture taken professionally?"

"No."

"I can do it for you. I'm a photographer. You should be on the front of a magazine with a bone structure like yours."

"Thanks." Taylor is only half listening. *She promised. She promised.* Creepy Crawly gives Taylor a slow smile that makes her suddenly look at him properly. She thinks about maggots under the skin.

"I'll do it for nothing if you like—it'll be a secret between us." Creepy Crawly has tiny gobbets of spittle that speckle his lips when he speaks.

"I'll have to check with my mum. Will you tell Kat I was here?" Taylor turns away. Stuff him and his bone structure. She's already locked tight with secrets. She doesn't need any more. Taylor walks back down the path. The sleet has peppered the ground with a thousand balls of ice. Her feet scrunch down on them as she walks. It seems like a long time before she hears the click of the door closing.

Now she's not sure what to do.

She's not sure what to feel.

Kat promised. She *promised*.

And then it hits Taylor that something must have gone wrong.

Kat must have got detention—or else she's held up somewhere.

Any minute now she'll come hurtling down Sandy Lane, out of breath and full of apology. Taylor glances round. There's no sign of her yet, and it's getting late. Probably the best thing is to go into town on her own, and Kat will probably catch up with her there.

And if she doesn't, Taylor could lend Kat the "Spend Spend Spend" card and she can do it tomorrow. She lets herself relax. Almost smiles to herself. She's managing to do it. She's being laid back and easy going.

As she heads for the town Taylor stops at a phone booth and tries Grandad's number.

There's no answer.

35

"What was the problem with them?" Dracula-woman takes the striped sports shirts from Taylor and flips them over. Taylor stands awkwardly, wishing she'd put her hair up, or worn the vanilla cream jacket. She can't possibly be looking eighteen now.

"They were a present for my best mates. Only I got the wrong sizes. I think I've lost touch with the sorts of things they wear." It surprises Taylor that she says this. She hadn't planned it. It seems to come out all on its own.

In the background Rikki Cavalier is singing "Baby Let Me Put Things Right."

Dracula-woman tears a form from a pad and scribbles on it. "Sign here." She hands Taylor a pen.

Dracula-woman's fingernails are painted bloodred.

Taylor's hand is shaking as she writes. She has to remember the way she did the signature last time. There is a corner of her that is shocked that she knows she needs to do this. She realizes she could learn to think like a criminal. She could learn to be devious and sly. Or perhaps she already is.

Dracula-woman take the form back, then hands a copy to Taylor.

She swipes the "Spend Spend Spend" card through the machine, and slides it back across the counter.

Taylor picks it up. Once Kat has brought back her stuff, they will destroy the card. Maybe they'll burn it with Kat's thin gold lighter. Taylor likes the idea of the card being a melted shapeless lump. It will be a monster tamed.

Dracula-woman is already carrying the sports shirts back to the rail.

It is all over. Finished. Within minutes the shirts will be hanging with all the others.

Taylor thinks they might have a kind of reunion.

"Hey—where did you lot get to?"

"Some girl's house. Not sure where."

"Lucky sods, getting out of this dump. Why d'you come back?"

"Dunno. Didn't quite fit, I s'pose." There is a rustle of sympathy, as if this is a danger for all new clothes.

Taylor turns to leave Fantasy. There is a row of dresses on a rail near the door. Taylor is drawn to them. She didn't notice them on her way in, but they look special. They're not quite real—they're magical Cinderella types—all long and floaty and sparkly bright. They're too old for Taylor—she'd need a padded bra for those necklines—but she loves the way the colours dance. She loves the way the skirts swirl. She picks out a pink one and holds it against her. It's unashamedly girlie—but it's wonderful. She won't try it on—she's not getting into that game again. Instead she makes a picture in her head. She calls the picture "School Ball," and has the dresses all giggling and blushing in clusters round the hall. The stripy sports shirts swagger about talking loudly, punching each other playfully, pretending not to look at the dresses.

"Baby Let Me Put Things Right" fades away.

There is a pause before the next song kicks in.

And in that pause Taylor hears a voice, huskily soft, saying, "I would have gone for that if I'd seen it. Are there any more?"

Another voice answers. "I don't think so. I think I got the last one."

"It's really great. Different."

Taylor can see blonde hair, long and silvery, through the gaps in the clothes rails. She can't quite make out who Kat's talking to, but she doesn't care. It doesn't matter.

Kat has kept her promise. She's bringing the stuff back.

Taylor pushes her way through the rails.

Kat has her back to her.

Taylor will do the nudge from behind—take Kat by surprise for once.

And then Taylor sees it—almost in slow motion.

The girl Kat has been talking to holds a dress up in front of her. The dress is lily white, with a soft green jacket. The girl—who looks younger than Taylor—is rose pink and happy. Flushed with excitement.

She has a fluffy yellow bag with a duck's face on it swinging from her shoulder.

Kat is standing behind her.

And then the film speeds up. Fast. Really fast. Swifter than a fish darting, Kat's hand is in the duck-face bag. Her fingers flash back out, holding a thin silver purse. She pushes the purse into her own school rucksack, and slips away.

36

Taylor grips the rail with the Cinderella dresses. She is swaying. Unsteady.

Memories swim out from behind all the rocks in her mind.

She is with Kat in the Top Marks changing room. They are laughing. Chewing gum. Kat has her makeup, and she is doing things to Taylor's face. Taylor stands trustingly. Stupidly. She closes her eyes, feeling Kat's touch on her lips. Her eyes. Her cheeks. Kat is laughing louder. She nudges Taylor in the back, and Taylor opens her eyes. Kat has given her a chalk-white face and huge blue lips. Silly pointed eyebrows. A round, red nose. Taylor turns her puzzled clown's eyes to Kat. Kat is laughing louder and louder, doubled up, her hands clutching her waist as if she has just heard the funniest joke in the world.

And suddenly Taylor isn't puzzled anymore.

Taylor feels sick. A sound escapes from somewhere

deep inside her. It is a thin watery whisper of pain.

She turns and stumbles out of the shop.

And it is only as she swerves left past the fountain that she realizes there is an alarm going off—a jagged endless wail of sound.

A security guard in a dark blue uniform is blocking her path.

And she still has the pink dress over her arm.

37

"Do you have to tell my mum?" Taylor is sitting at one side of a huge oak table in the upstairs office. On the wall is a poster which says "Dreams are free at Fantasy." A cloudy-haired girl with huge dark eyes and white white skin stares out mysteriously from a misty background. The poster is torn on one corner.

"We've already rung her. It's company policy." The security guard is sitting opposite Taylor.

"She's . . . she's not very well."

"She'll be even worse now."

From downstairs comes the muffled sound of Rikki Cavalier singing "How Did We Go So Wrong?"

"What will happen to me?"

The security guard knots his fingers together and clicks each one slowly.

Taylor notices that he has hairy hands. One of his fingers has a pale band of skin, as if he has only recently stopped wearing a ring. "Depends."

"It's my first time." Taylor has given up telling him it was all a mistake. She was telling him that outside by the fountain, and all the way up the stairs. He wasn't listening.

Now he glances across at her. He has hairy nostrils, too. Taylor wonders what his feet are like. "First time caught, you mean," he says.

Taylor thinks about the Nerd ramming his bike up against the climbing frame.

Tinker, tailor, soldier, sailor,
Rich man, poor man, beggar man, . . .

Taylor cuts the rhyme off in her head. She can't imagine how Mum is going to get here.

Will the police bring her?

Will she arrive in the beige dressing gown?

She thinks about Mum getting the knock on the door: *"Excuse me, madam, but there's been a bit of an incident."* Inspector Whizz would never use a word like "incident."

She looks round as the door opens.

A policeman walks in.

He is followed by Grandad.

Taylor has her head in her hands.

Words are passing backwards and forwards across her. She's not listening. She can't listen. She is tired. She feels distant and fuzzy and far, far away.

At some time—Taylor doesn't notice when—the policeman and the security guard leave the room.

Grandad touches her shoulder and says, "We'll sort this out."

"I thought you were ill." Taylor doesn't want to look at him. She is sorry—so sorry—that he has been dragged into this.

"I've told you before—I'm tough as old boots." Grandad slides the security guard's chair nearer to Taylor. "It was just a bug. A twenty-four-hour thing. Mrs. Parker made such a fuss about me, I thought I'd better drive down to see you, just to let you know I wasn't really at death's door."

Taylor makes her eyes focus on him.

He's not quite okay. She can see this on him like a faint shadowed outline. But his eyes are smiling.

"You can shout at me if you want," she says.

"I don't want."

"I didn't nick it. It was a mistake."

"I know."

"How do you know?"

"Because I know you," says Grandad gently.

Taylor looks away.

Her heart is stinging. She imagines it as a blob of blue jelly, a strange sea creature drifting past. It scrapes against rocks. The soft pulp of it is torn. Sadness leaks from it, seeping into the waves like swirly blue ink.

The heart in the "This Is Your Body" poster is blue.

Taylor shakes her head. "I never told you," she whispers. "I never told you how it happened."

Grandad squeezes her shoulder. "Then maybe it's time you did."

39

"*I wish she'd stop doing that.*" *Taylor shields her eyes against the sudden shower of sand as Laura digs out the moat round her castle with a spade.*

"*Take her in the water then.*" *Mum doesn't lift her head from the sunbed she is lying on. "You could probably both do with cooling off."*

"*She can't swim.*" *Taylor watches Laura squash a rainbow-striped rabbit on top of the castle. She makes the toy dance, singing "I'm the king of the castle" in a high squeaky voice.*

Taylor sighs. She doesn't want Laura tagging along with her. She wants to go in the sea on her own. She wants to go round to the rocky bit on the other side. She wants to look for giant shells, like the ones they sell in the gift shop. She saw them on the first day they arrived, when they went in to buy the inflatable boat.

"*Go on. Just for ten minutes.*" *Mum does raise her head slightly this time, pulling her sunglasses down and* looking at Taylor over the top of them. "This is my holiday too, sweetheart. Give me a bit of peace."

"Please please please, Taylor." Laura has stopped making the rabbit dance and rolls sideways onto the inflatable boat. The inflatable boat gives a belch of noise like a fart. Laura giggles, poking the pattern of white printed sea horses that prance round the edge. "The sea horses had beans for breakfast."

Taylor raises her eyes to the sky. "How come six-year-olds have so much energy?" she grumbles.

"It'll be worth an ice cream when you come back." Mum settles back onto the sunbed and turns her face the other way.

Taylor sifts sand through her fingers, and feels the sun pour down on her. This is the first holiday abroad that they've had since Dad did what Mum always called his "Great Disappearing Act." He's been gone since Laura was a baby. When he first went she imagined him reappearing suddenly, magically, like a proper magician. And even now, she thinks of him as someone in a cloak and a big top hat. Although the truth is that she hardly thinks of him at all.

"Go on, Taylor." Laura pokes her with the paw of the rainbow-striped rabbit. "You can have my ice cream as well if you take me."

"Oh wow," says Taylor. Then she shrugs. If she does this for Mum now, she can go round the rocks later. They're here for another four days and it's not as if the weather's going to change or anything.

She jumps up, grabbing the rope that is attached to one end of the boat.

Laura gives a squeal of excitement.

Taylor scowls at her. "No squealing. It's too embarrassing."

Taylor doesn't remember if Mum says anything as they leave. She doesn't remember if Mum tells her to be careful. She doesn't remember if Mum says good-bye to Laura. Or if Laura says good-bye to Mum.

They probably don't.

They wouldn't have known that they needed to.

Grandad touches Taylor's hand. "Are you okay?" he speaks softly.

Taylor stares down at where his fingers are squeezing hers. She squeezes back, but she doesn't look at him. She can't. She daren't.

Taylor goes in up to her knees, dragging the boat behind her. Laura scrambles in and Taylor swings it round.

Laura squeals, "Faster."

"Stop squealing," says Taylor.

She gets behind the boat, pushing it forwards with both hands. The water laps over it, covering the prancing white sea horses. Then it nudges up onto a sand bank and stops.

"Boring!" Laura splashes Taylor. "Go deeper."

Taylor is still only up to her knees, but she knows this

bit of the sea stays shallow. She walked for ages yester-
day and the water just touched her belly. She can't face
going that far and dragging a squealing Laura behind her.

Over to her left are the rocks. She explored them yes-
terday, too, and she knows that even there it is not that
deep. Only up to her shoulders, and only in places.

She swings sideways, running suddenly, the weight of
the water hitting the fronts of her thighs. The seabed here
is flat and warm. Taylor's toes sink down into its softness.
She is running through fudge. Taylor glances round at
Laura. Laura has her hands stretched out on either side of
the boat, her fingertips dancing in the water. Her blonde
curls have been splashed by the spray, and are twizzled
tight as corkscrews. She is laughing, her whole face lit up.

They reach the rocks, and Taylor spins the boat round
again, only more carefully this time. She doesn't want to
scrape the rough stone.

The water laps past her chest now. It is deep enough
for her to swim. She paddles gently, one hand still guiding
the boat. It's cooler out here, and the sea is very clear.
Laura lies faceup. She is singing softly. "Row, row, row
your boat, gently down the stream . . ."

A seagull circles slowly.

The beach, bright with colour, is a long way off.

"I wish we could stay here forever," says Taylor.

"I don't." Laura splashes her lazily. "I want my ice
cream."

"You said I could have it." Taylor splashes her back.

Laura sticks her tongue out. "Meanie," she says. "You'll get fat."

Taylor treads water, the way they learnt in Junior School swimming lessons. She is moving backwards, pulling the boat out deeper.

Looking down, the sea is like blue glass. There are rocks along the bottom, their shapes uncertain in the dappled light. Ripples of coloured plants are moving, swaying. The sun spills into the water, catching on shoals of tiny fish that dart out suddenly, first one way, and then the other. They are beautiful. Lit golden. Like living treasure. Taylor thinks she will get one of those snorkel things from the gift shop and come back later for a proper look.

She turns slightly, pushing at the boat with her elbow. She has to be careful they don't drift too far. She can still touch the bottom with her toes.

In the staff room at Fantasy, Grandad is still gripping Taylor's hand.

Taylor clings to the quiet strength of him. His strength is keeping her in one piece. It is stopping her from becoming just the scraps of a picture that no one would ever want to put together again.

"You don't have to do the next bit. Not if you don't want to."

Taylor shakes her head. Images wash over her. "I have to," she whispers. But she isn't sure if she can do it. Not all of it. Not exactly as it happened. If Grandad knew everything he might snatch his quiet strength away.

Taylor's foot brushes the rough edge of one of the rocks.

And suddenly she squeals. Something sharp, something stinging, is biting into the sole of her foot. She twists sideways, trying to raise her leg to get a look. She isn't just treading water now. She is swimming properly. She jabs at the boat, shoving it towards the shore. The pain is filling her foot. Her ankle. Taylor pictures it all swelling, poisonous. She thinks about amputation. And it is only then that she realizes the boat has gone light. Easy to push. And empty.

L aura is swirling down, down, down. Her twizzled hair spreads and floats like a strange sea star. Taylor dives, although she isn't any good at diving. She keeps her eyes open, and they sting. She grabs at Laura, praying Laura will hold on to her. She doesn't. She just drifts on downwards, resting on the bottom, stirring up soft white sand so that it flurries round her like a mist. Taylor grabs her again, her grip firmer this time. Laura is made of stone. Taylor's legs graze the edges of rocks. There is a pain in her chest. The effort is huge.

And then suddenly she bursts through the skin of the water. The hot bright golden sun burns down onto her. The sea glitters and sparkles. The boat is only metres away.

Taylor struggles towards it.

She'll get Laura on it, and get them back to the beach and it will be all right.

They'll chatter about this tonight, over pizza and salad in the taverna.

Later, as the warm night folds over them, they'll order ice cream. Strawberry ones. Taylor won't have hers. She'll give it to Laura. She'll ask the waiter to put a sparkler in it.

Laura likes sparklers.

"Somehow I got us to the beach." Taylor's voice is heavy. Flat. "I think I was running. I might have been crying. Other people came over . . ."

She breaks off.

Grandad has pulled her close now, stroking her hair. "It was an accident." He grips her tighter. "It wasn't your fault."

Taylor isn't listening. She wants to talk. She *has* to talk. She has to get to the end. "There was a crowd of people, all pushing round us. A man started leaning over Laura. I didn't want him there. I thought she'd be frightened when she woke up, so I shouted at him. I might have even hit him. Someone got hold of me, and pulled me away. And then Mum was beside me and she was asking me what was wrong and she didn't realize at first and she thought it was somebody else and she kept saying how terrible, and what an awful thing to happen on holiday, and I couldn't speak and she said, 'Where's Laura?'—and then she started to scream. . . ."

41

The policeman comes in.

He looks at Taylor's puffy eyes and at Grandad stroking Taylor's hair. "I think you've learnt your lesson," he says. "The store manager has agreed that he won't press charges, but I need you to know that we do now have your name on file. If you ever come to our attention again . . ."

He lets Grandad lead Taylor down the stairs.

The shop is closed, and Dracula-woman has to come and unlock the door.

Outside in the precinct the water fountain is turned off.

The security guard is collecting the pennies with a net.

They head for Betsy. Grandad keeps one hand on Taylor's arm as they walk, as if he is afraid of what will happen if he lets go.

• • •

"Home, safe and sound." Grandad puts the key in the front door, and they step inside.

Mum is hovering in the hall. Her face is ghost pale.

Taylor thinks about the pictures they used to do at infants' school. Chalk-white faces on dark paper backgrounds.

"You haven't got your coat," says Mum. "You must be frozen."

Taylor stares at Mum. Her eyes ache. Her throat aches. She puts her hand over the smear of muted brown paint on her sleeve. "I'm fine," she mumbles.

"I think we should talk." Mum is following Taylor through the hall, up the stairs.

"I don't want to."

"No—not now." Mum says this very gently, as if Taylor is a frightened stray kitten who has to have food left outside in the snow. Slowly, day by day, the food will be edged nearer the house. Slowly, day by day, the kitten will get brave enough to edge nearer the house with it. "But, I just want you to know—it's been a rough ride for you. I've been a mess, and I've let you down."

Taylor looks back at Mum. Her chalk-white face has smoky grey smudges under her eyes. Taylor remembers what it was like, smudging chalk with her fingers. She can remember coming home from school, clutching "Mummy and Me" and crying. She was crying because she had got chalk smears on the sleeve of her school blouse.

She expected Mum to be cross, but she wasn't. She hugged Taylor and looked at "Mummy and Me" and said it was the best picture ever. She hung it on the fridge, fixing it with a magnet shaped like a tomato. And in the morning the smears were gone from the blouse, and Taylor had almost forgotten they were ever there.

And now Taylor wants to tell Mum that she hasn't let her down.

It is only Taylor who has done the wrong thing. The terrible thing.

But Mum doesn't know that, because there's something Taylor hasn't told her.

Something Taylor hasn't told Grandad.

Something Taylor has hardly dared to tell herself.

She reaches the door to her room. "I want to be on my own for a while," she says.

Mum nods.

The kitten won't even sniff the food.

42

Taylor sits on her bed. She doesn't want to think about Mum. Or Grandad. Or Laura. She's said too much—but she hasn't said enough.

She gets up off the bed again. She pulls drawers out, flattening out knickers that didn't need flattening, folding up jumpers that didn't need folding. She fusses by the dressing table, rearranges a few things, then puts them back in the same place again. She leaves out the silver foil wrapper and the lilac shimmer lipstick. Later, when she goes downstairs, she will chuck them in the bin.

Tucked in the frame of the dressing table mirror she spots the photo booth pictures of her and Kat.

She takes them down. Kat still looks like Kat, but there is something different about her now. Taylor can see a hard edge that she never saw before. Kat looks sharper. More pointed. Taylor wonders how she could have been so blind. So stupid.

Suddenly she goes to her box under the bed. She pulls out scissors and glue, and a square of white card.

She gets the foil wrapper, rolling it into seven thin sticks. With the lipstick she draws a body onto the card. It is a lumpy cartoony shape with lilac splodges. She glues on five of the foil sticks, making four legs and a tail. She positions the legs at right angles to the body—two going frontways, and two going back.

Next she cuts Kat's face out, choosing the picture where Kat looks worst. She glues this down, then fixes the last two sticks onto the forehead. She twists them so that they curl out from the paper. Horns.

Underneath she prints the words "Lying Cow."

And then suddenly, from Laura's room, she hears something.

Taylor drops "Lying Cow."

It falls silently onto the carpet.

She doesn't notice the scrunch of it under her feet as she leaves the room.

Laura's door is open.

The light is on.

The cobwebs are broken.

Taylor stands, staring in. She feels puzzled that it all looks the same. Except for the dust. Somehow she had expected it to be darker. More scary.

Mum is sitting on Laura's bed. She looks up at

Taylor. "Grandad's asleep in my room. He looks washed out, but he's eaten a bit. He seems to be okay."

"What are you doing in here?"

"Just sitting. Just thinking. I haven't touched anything. I've just turned the radiator on. It's freezing."

Taylor walks in slowly.

The pink flower quilt is still on Laura's bed, as if she might come bouncing in, jump up on it, snuggle under it.

Her toys are there too, lined up on the end of the bed.

A memory Taylor doesn't want pushes into her head. It is Laura, packing. She is taking forever. Mum has told her she can only take one cuddly on holiday. Laura is picking them up one by one, trying to choose which one to take. And worse—heartbreakingly worse—which ones to leave.

Taylor is saying, "It's only a week. You'll see them again in a week."

"But it's not fair," Laura says, in a voice that is younger than six. "The ones I don't take will be upset. They'll think I don't love them."

"Life's not fair." Taylor is so old. So wise. "I'll tell you what though—give one to me to pack. I'm not taking anything of mine, so that way you'll get to take two."

"Are you sure?" Laura is unbelieving. How can Taylor not want to take her own cuddly?

"As long as you're quick." Taylor pretends to sigh. "If you dither too long I might change my mind."

With a bounce of excitement Laura plucks out the chosen two.

They are a rainbow-striped rabbit called Fluff, and a one-eared bear called Oscar.

Then she flings herself at Taylor, hugging her as if she has given her the world.

Taylor, who is far too old for this sort of thing, untangles her gently and pushes her away.

Taylor looks suddenly at Mum. "Do you hate me?"

Mum looks straight back at her. "I love you," she says.

"I know something that will make you hate me. Something about what really happened with Laura. Something I didn't tell you."

"Tell me now," says Mum.

Taylor walks over to Laura's window.

It is a clear, cold night.

The stars glitter, beautiful and distant, against the wash of black.

The green flashing light of an aeroplane winks its way across the silence.

Taylor closes her eyes, and picks her way backwards through more memories she doesn't want to have.

43

Taylor is gazing down through an underwater fairy-land. Plants sway and swirl. Their long tentacled leaves are tinted pinks and blues. Tiny rainbow fish swim out from behind them, swarming like clouds of butterflies.

"I want to go back," says Laura, peering over the side of the boat.

"In a minute." Taylor can't pull her gaze away. "You've had a good time. Now you have to wait for me."

"But it looks deep." Laura begins to sit up in the boat. It tips slightly, water sloshing in. "Yeuck. That water's cold."

"Stop it," says Taylor. "Just keep still. I've seen something."

Sparkling up through the liquid blue are a million stars.

They are everywhere. The glow of them seems to stretch forever, twinkling silver amongst the forests of swaying weeds. "Stay there," says Taylor. "I'm going to try and get something."

"Where could I go?" Laura's voice is whiny. Taylor knows it won't be long before she becomes a pain.

But this will only take a second. She just has to dive fast, grab a handful of stars, and come back up.

She can't dive properly—she's never liked getting water in her eyes—but she might never see anything like this again. She wants to own this moment of magic. Treasure it forever. Take it home and keep it on her dressing table. Taylor jabs the boat, pushing it towards shallower water. Then she takes a deep breath, and goes for the stars.

"I grabbed a handful, but as soon as I touched them, they disappeared. They were nothing. Not real. A trick of the light. All I was holding were cold strands of seaweed. And it was then that my foot touched the rock." Taylor opens her eyes again. "I knew about sea anemones—that holiday rep warned us—but the stars were so magical. I forgot to be careful. The thing stung me. It was spiky. Agony. Every time I kicked, its spines moved under my skin. I kept thinking about how I was being poisoned. I came up too fast under the boat. It tipped . . ."

Outside, another aeroplane passes, travelling the other way.

She waits for Mum to do something. To shake her

or to scream. To storm from the room and slam the door. Taylor imagines Mum leaving her locked in with Laura's pink flowered bed quilt, buried forever amongst the cuddly toys.

And then Mum's arm is round her and Taylor is saying, "I'm sorry. I'm sorry." And she is crying for the first time since it happened, and it is like the whole hard shell of her is splitting open, and the real Taylor is uncurling at last.

44

"You can skip school today." Mum comes in from the garden carrying a small cluster of snowdrops.

Taylor glances up from her Supa Shoppa breakfast cereal. "I have to go in," she says.

Mum hangs her jacket over the back of the chair and starts arranging the snowdrops in a vase. "Grandad's still in bed at the moment, but he's taking me shopping later this morning. I . . . I thought maybe—if we feel up to it—we could all go out to lunch together."

Taylor shifts uncomfortably in her chair, and stirs the Supa Shoppa breakfast cereal slowly round the bowl. Some of it gets pushed to the side and Taylor makes a dotted puff pattern on the white china. Mum still looks tired, but the chalk and shadows have gone from her face. She's really trying. She thinks everything's getting sorted. "I can't miss school," Taylor says. "There's some stuff I haven't got finished. I'll be in trouble if I don't get on with it."

This is almost true.

Although it's not schoolwork that Taylor is talking about.

Taylor is going back to Kat's.

The new split-open Taylor will get those clothes off her even if she has to ransack Kat's room herself.

She will take the stuff back to the shops on her own.

She won't have to worry Mum about "Spend Spend Spend."

And once the card is paid back, she will never need to talk to Kat again.

Pushing her breakfast to one side, she makes a show of glancing at the kitchen clock. "I'd better get going," she says. "Otherwise I'll end up with detention."

Five minutes later she is outside Kat's house, knocking on Kat's front door.

"You again?" Kat's mum opens the door. She is blinking, as if the morning light hurts her eyes.

"Kat's borrowed something of mine and I need it back." The new Taylor doesn't hover and make excuses like yesterday. The new Taylor knows what she wants.

Kat's mum gives a harsh laugh, then winces, as if the sound hurts her too. "You'll never find anything in that room of hers."

She turns away, wandering back down the hall as if

she suddenly can't be bothered. She has left the door open though. The new Taylor takes this as an invitation to go in.

She hurries up to Kat's room.

She *almost* doesn't knock, but then decides this might be taking things too far. Inspector Whizz would always knock on the door before he broke it down.

She knocks softly, and then louder. There is no answer.

Taking a deep breath, Taylor slowly turns the handle, opens the door, and steps into the room.

"Not again." Kat blinks at Taylor and struggles to sit up in bed. She looks washed out. Her eyes are smudged grey with last night's mascara. Taylor notices for the first time that there are dark roots in her hair.

"I waited for you yesterday, by the gate." Taylor finds she is shaking. It was easy to practise this fighting talk in her imagination. It is not so easy now.

Kat swings her legs over the side of the bed, stretches and yawns. "Bloody detention," she says. "I came looking for you afterwards. I even went into town."

It's a blow to Taylor that Kat has got the town bit in first. That was going to be her golden moment—the bit when she pulls back the curtain, the Truth standing like some sort of Triumphant Knight, his sword pointing at Kat's heart.

Kat smiles. The smile seems to knock something out of Taylor too. It is so friendly. So open. Best mates.

Taylor makes a picture in her mind of Kat's fingers round the silver purse.

She isn't going to mention it—Kat would be bound to wriggle out of it with some story or other—but it's a weapon in Taylor's head. The best defense she's got. Taylor makes the picture bigger. Brighter. She holds it in her mind like a shield. "I need those clothes today," she says. "We've got to get them back after school."

She waits for the excuses to come dancing out like naughty children.

Kat nods. "They're here." She takes down a carrier bag that is hooked over the rail, and touches Taylor's arm. Her eyes are warm. Beautiful. Regretful. "I won't be able to come with you though. I'm busy tonight. Mum wants Wayne—that's her boyfriend—to take some new pictures of me. I'm really really sorry."

Awkwardly Taylor fumbles with the bag, looking inside so that she doesn't have to look at Kat.

"It's all there," says Kat.

"I just—I couldn't remember exactly what you'd bought. I thought I'd better check." This isn't true. Taylor has the "Spend Spend Spend" receipts. She knows what Kat bought down to the very last button.

"Look, I'm not being funny or anything, but I need to get dressed. That detention yesterday—it was because I was late in." Kat doesn't add "because of you," but she may as well.

Taylor almost nods. She almost leaves quickly,

scuttling away. She doesn't have to see this through to the death. She can get out of here and sort it on her own—and just keep clear of Kat for ever and ever. She feels muddled suddenly about how much of this mess Kat has planned, and how much just sort of happened. Could Kat really have picked her out, that first day in Glitzie's? Could she really have seen that Taylor would be that easy to fool?

Part of her wants to make excuses. It is so hard to let the old Kat go. But the silver purse flashes a warning in Taylor's head again. And now another purse pushes into her mind. Tiger striped. Fluffy. A different purse. A different bag. But the same fingers closing round it. The same hand sneaking it out.

And Taylor's fighting voice says, "It won't take a minute—save me coming back." And she empties the carrier bag onto the bed.

Everything is creased and rumpled. It looks like a load of stuff for a jumble sale. "I can't take it back like this."

Kat goes to the dressing table mirror and examines a blotch on her chin. "I'll iron it then," she sighs. "It's only been in that bag."

Taylor holds up the yellow silk jacket. "This looks like you've slept in it." She pulls out the red chiffon dress, the "leather look" skirt and top. "And this. And this. You must have worn it all." Her voice is sharpening. The fighting talk is smashing its way out of her, fists clenched, looking for trouble.

Kat picks up a can called "A Touch of Blonde" and sprays it onto her hair. "I haven't worn it. Not properly anyway."

"What d'you mean, not properly?"

Kat rubs the spray into her roots. "I practised for a photo session last night. I went through it with Mum. I only wore each thing for a few minutes."

Taylor is hardly listening. She is examining everything. A loose thread here. A smudge of lipstick there. She holds up the yellow silk jacket, turning it towards the light. It is stained—splotched with a scatter of dark spots. "This looks like . . . like . . ." She wrinkles her nose, then forces herself to sniff it. ". . . red wine."

Kat starts putting on lipstick. "Tell the shop you don't know anything about it. They won't care. They'll just send it back to the manufacturer. Everyone—"

Taylor grips the jacket tightly. She wants to rip it to pieces. She wants to rip Kat to pieces. "I'm *not* taking it back." She bites her lips, counting to ten. "I'll have to tell my mum. She'll have to know everything."

Kat's voice is suddenly steel hard. It is a voice Taylor would never have recognized across a shop floor. "Getting stuff through false pretences is illegal. You've got nothing on me. It's your name on that card."

Taylor feels a rushing in her chest. She is about to

charge towards something unknown. Uncertain. But she doesn't care. "I *want* my mum to know. I'm getting this over with."

She pushes the clothes back in the carrier bag, shoving them in. It doesn't matter. They're messed up anyway. As she pushes at the door she turns. "I expect my mum will be round to see yours."

Kat drops the lipstick with a clatter and springs between Taylor and the door. She raises her arm. Taylor thinks she is going to hit her. She thinks there is really going to be a fight.

And then Kat's whole face seems to crumble. "Please." Her voice is trembling. "Please don't tell your mum about me."

"Tell me one good reason why I shouldn't."

For a moment they both stare at each other.

And in that moment Taylor sees the armour of Kat begin to crack open. There are layers and layers of her. The cool confident funny Kat. The beautiful magical wonderful Kat. The best mate share-all-your-secrets Kat. The dark mysterious secretive Kat. The hard sly devious Kat.

And now the layers are being stripped away. The Kat in the middle is just small and scared and shrinking from the light. "Just hear me out for five minutes," she says.

45

"I'm not going to have to be like this forever." Kat stands in the middle of a pile of clothes. "It's just that—right now I can't stop. I daren't stop. I have to have new stuff. I have to keep trying."

Taylor still has her fingers on the door handle. She has at least learned *some* lessons. She knows she is a soft touch. She knows she can be easily fooled. "It's only clothes," she says. "I can't see how you can make clothes *that* important." She wants to add "more important than friends" but she stops herself. She doesn't want to sound as if it matters.

"My mum never wanted me." Kat says this in a small, thin voice that Taylor has never heard before.

"Wanted you to do what?" Taylor can't work out what she means.

Kat turns away suddenly, and goes to the bottom drawer of her dressing table. She thrusts a gold-framed photograph at Taylor.

Taylor steps forwards reluctantly, and stares at it. "You look—different," she says at last. She wants to say "softer." "Sweeter." But she doesn't.

"That's because it isn't me. It's Mum. About my age."

Taylor looks at the picture again and nods. She can see it now. It is nearly Kat, but not quite.

Kat traces the frame with her finger. "She had everything. She was going for the top. It was like a fairy-tale world opening up for her. And then she got pregnant."

"With you?"

Kat stuffs the photograph back in the bottom drawer. "With me."

"But . . ." Taylor shrugs. She wants to say "So what?" but she changes it to, "What's so terrible about that?"

"After she had me, nobody booked her. She didn't get any modelling work. Her moment had come, and gone, and I'd got in the middle of it. I'd buggered it up."

Taylor twists the handles of the carrier bag. She knows about guilt. She thinks she should try to understand. But Kat's world is so small. She sees Kat and her mum as flimsy. Made of tissue paper. They will blow away in the thinnest breeze. She wonders suddenly what they would do if something really bad ever happened to them. They would be ripped away into scraps of nothing. They would never be seen again.

She hears something breaking downstairs.

Kat is staring into the dressing-table mirror. "She

threw her energy into me instead. All her dreams for herself got hooked on to me. I was always being booked up. I had the look. The cute curls and big eyes and everything. Mum was really proud of me. But now . . . but now . . ." Kat's voice trails off. She snatches up a Raspberry Pink lipstick and draws a face in front of her reflection. She gives it long rippling hair. She presses so hard, the lipstick breaks. She drops it back down onto the dressing table.

Taylor longs to go, but Kat keeps talking.

"Wayne says I'm not what the agents are after. He says I'm not the face of the moment. He says I'm not different enough. And I'm too pretty. Can you believe that? Too *pretty!*"

Taylor can hear someone crying downstairs. She swallows another "So what?"

"Mum doesn't agree with him. She and Wayne row and row about it. She says it's his fault. He's not doing the pictures right. And we're running out of time. If I don't make it in the next year or two, it'll be too late."

"Well—then you'll do something else, surely?"

"I was brought up for this. Mum let me miss loads of school and everything, when I was little. She always said it was more important to groom me for shoots and stuff." She picks up some Wild Red nail varnish and begins splodging spots onto the lipstick face. "And I don't want anything else. Neither does Mum. It's doing her in, me not getting work . . ." Grabbing a silver glitter hair gel she holds it high above her head, as if she is going to throw it. But she doesn't throw it. Instead she sprays giant crosses onto the mirror, going over and over the lipstick face.

Then she turns to Taylor. Her eyes are desperate. Pleading. "That's why you mustn't say anything about that card thing. If you tell your mum, we don't know what she'll do. I might end up with a police record. Then I won't stand a chance with the modelling. I'll be finished. And Mum will be too."

Taylor feels trapped. She still wants her mum to know. She still wants it sorted properly. But she knows what it's like to need to keep secrets. And she doesn't want to be the finishing of Kat or Kat's mum.

Kat steps towards Taylor. "Don't wreck everything. It's rough enough here. My aunt Bev says . . ."

Taylor clutches the carrier bag, and steps back from Kat. "I thought she was dead."

"I . . ." Kat gives a nervous laugh, and her eyes won't meet Taylor's. "I got it wrong. Mum must have got muddled about it. It was her that said . . ."

And it is this that does it for Taylor. This is bigger than all the other stuff. Bigger than Kat taking Taylor for a fool. Bigger than her nicking the tiger-striped purse. Taylor knows that Kat will lie about somebody being dead just to get what she wants.

But instead of a fresh wave of anger, Taylor feels stronger suddenly. As if she is waking up.

And she feels older than Kat.

Older than Kat's mum.

She will have to sort this "Spend Spend Spend" stuff on her own. She never ever ever wants anything more to do with Kat.

As she slips from the room she passes Kat's mum, slumped near the bottom of the stairs.

And it seems to Taylor that Kat's mum is nearly finished already.

46

"A hundred pounds?" Mum puts down the potato peeler and takes the "Spend Spend Spend" card from Taylor. She turns it over in her hand. "I'd forgotten I'd even applied for it."

"Not quite a hundred. I didn't get through the lot." Taylor stares out of the window. The snow has gone completely now, and the afternoon sky is a wash of watery blue. She is waiting for Mum to throw saucepans or plates or potato peelings at her. Perhaps Kat is right. Perhaps she will even call the police and have Taylor taken away. Perhaps that is the best thing for her. "I'm sorry."

Mum folds the "Spend Spend Spend" card across the middle. It bends but it doesn't snap. "I'm sorry too."

"I'll get a job. A paper round or something." Taylor thinks that Mum looks more sad than angry. This makes her feel worse.

"We'll sort it out. But it scares me that you did something like that. You must have known it was illegal. If you'd got caught . . ." Mum shakes her head. "I can't believe you did something so stupid on your own. That girl Kat? The one who went shopping with you last week . . . ?"

Taylor stares down at her hands. She won't lie again. She just won't say anything.

Mum makes her lips go very thin. "I think I'd better talk to Kat's parents."

"I don't think her dad lives with them," says Taylor. "Her mum's got some creepy bloke called Wayne instead."

"And how much was this girl involved? How much did she encourage you?"

Taylor looks up at Mum. "Please leave her out of it. Going to her mum won't do any good, and it might do some bad."

Mum sharpens. "You mean Kat would bully you?"

"No. Nothing like that." Taylor watches a robin land on the roof of the Wendy House. "It's just—they're such a mess—all of them. You'd never get through and—it's my name on that card." She's not trying to protect Kat. Kat did something that has cut deep into her. But now that it's done she wants it over with. She doesn't want to spend the rest of her life picking at the scab.

Mum bends the card the other way. It still doesn't

snap, but a thin white crack appears down the middle. "But Kat's mum *should* know. Any mother would want to know."

A vision of Kat's mum looms up in Taylor's head. A creature unlike any other. "She's not like you. She's not like any mother. For a while I thought Kat was a bit like me but . . ." She pauses, then says slowly, "I was wrong."

Mum looks hard at Taylor for a moment, then sighs. "Well, I guess we'll just sort it out between us. We've been through so much. This is big, but it's not huge."

"What . . . what about the clothes? I've got them all in my room still."

"Well, I can't take them back. Apart from anything else, I've just destroyed the card. The shops would need to swipe it before they'd give us a refund." Mum frowns for a moment. "Is there anything you'd want to wear?"

Taylor thinks about the yellow silk jacket. The red chiffon dress. The "leather look" skirt and top. It's all Kat's image. Kat's dream. Kat's nightmare. She shakes her head. "Nothing," she says.

"We'll take them all to a charity shop then."

"You mean—just give them away?" Taylor thinks about all that money. All that waste.

"Somebody may as well get the use out of them." Mum smiles suddenly. "It might make some young girl's day—discovering that lot amongst the fusty old blouses and granny cardigans. Think of it like that. And for us . . . we'll put it all down to experience, and just start again. A new beginning."

Taylor rolls the words over and over in her head. *A new beginning. A new beginning.* She watches the robin flutter to the top of the swing. It looks as if the cobwebs have all been brushed away. Grandad insisted on clearing the garden before he went back last night. They'd tried to make him stay—Mum thought he needed to rest—but he'd said he couldn't risk Monty with Mrs. Parker any longer. "I like that idea," Taylor says at last. "I like the thought of a new beginning."

Mum touches her shoulder. "You've changed so much. I'm sorry if I made you grow up too fast. I'm sorry I didn't deal with things properly. But we're getting it sorted now. Together. We won't need cheap friends or pills or any other rubbish." She bends the "Spend Spend Spend" card again. This time it does snap. A clean break. Mum puts the two halves in the pile of potato peelings. "I'll throw it all away in a minute," she says.

Outside, the robin swoops across to the rose bush. Taylor notices there are already buds on the tips of the branches.

47

It is Saturday morning.

Taylor is in her bedroom, making "Laura's Dream."

It's the first proper collage she's done for ages. She's using things that are Laura's—bits of things that it feels all right to cut up. She has started thinking that Laura might still be around. Sometimes she gets a sense of her. Sometimes she almost sees her. None of this is scary. Taylor likes thinking of Laura being close. She hopes she is feeling peaceful, and safe.

"Laura's Dream" has a sweetness about it, a softness that seems to float out without Taylor properly understanding how it is happening. It is a garden of flowers. A paradise glimpsed through a hazy misted sky. As Taylor works, she realizes that Kat was right about one thing: She *is* lucky. Nobody can take this from her.

She lets her mind roll on, daydreaming about a future where she is Queen of Collage. She will sell pictures. Have exhibitions in big London galleries. She may do stories to go with her pictures too, really honest ones that say something about what she felt at the time. She thinks that people will like this. People always need to make sense of things.

She rummages through her box, searching for really special bits and pieces. She will write a story for "Laura's Dream" too. It'll be the first collage to have a story. It will make it even more special.

Downstairs the phone rings.

A moment later Mum comes up. "That was for you."

Taylor pulls out a white silk ribbon. "Who was it?"

"Sam and Sophie."

Taylor twiddles the white silk ribbon. She finds that if she cuts a snip at one end, the rest tears in a thin curl along the length of it. She thinks that thin, white curls will be just right for petals. "What did they want?"

"To go shopping. With you."

"I'm too busy."

"I'll let you have some money—you won't need to feel like you're just following them around."

Taylor opens her fingers and lets the white curled petals drift down onto the paper. She wants to let them choose where they will settle. "I already owe you nearly two hundred quid."

"You know I'm going back to work next week. We'll be able to sort that out."

"I need to get this finished. I've got loads of ideas for it. I might forget them if I stop now."

"Taylor—" Mum walks over and kneels besides her. It is unexpected.

Taylor feels awkward. She's not used to letting anyone watch her work. "What?"

"It's a beautiful picture. I want to frame it and hang it downstairs when it's finished. It'll be a celebration of Laura. But you need a break. You need to get out with your friends."

"I don't *want* to go out with Sam and Sophie." Taylor wants to add that they're not friends now. It all got ruined. But she doesn't say this because she doesn't want to give Mum anything new to worry about.

"Well—I've already said that you'll go," says Mum, standing up. "They're going to be here in half an hour. Why don't you get changed? You can finish your picture when you get back."

Taylor drops the remains of the white silk ribbon back into the box. She doesn't want to get changed for Sam and Sophie. She wants to stay in her scruffy jeans and sweatshirt. But she is in the wrong mood for working on "Laura's Dream" now, so she might as well do something. Perhaps she'll keep the jeans and just change her top. Maybe she'll even wear the vanilla cream jacket. It'll be wasted if she doesn't. It'll end up in the bag for the charity shop.

But she wishes Mum wouldn't interfere with her life.

And she wishes Sam and Sophie would leave her alone.

Taylor gets up as Mum opens the door. A white silk petal has stuck to Taylor's sleeve, and she brushes her hand against it. It floats slowly down and settles on the carpet. Taylor watches it for a moment.

Then she shakes her head, like someone half remembering a dream, and follows Mum out of the room.

48

Sam and Sophie steer Taylor into Glitzie's.

The same signs are up.

LAST FEW REMAINING

REDUCED FOR ONE WEEK ONLY

HURRY WHILE STOCKS LAST

The clothes are different though. Taylor thinks there is probably a new, not-to-be-missed, special bargain offer every week.

The pop music seems louder than ever. Rikki Cavalier is punching out "Time to Start Over."

They walk past another display of "Buy One—Get One Free" lipsticks. This time it is glittery gold, and silver. Taylor can't imagine wanting gold or silver lips. And then she realizes that's why they're on offer. No one else wants them either.

Sam and Sophie don't stop to look at anything.

This surprises Taylor.

She had expected to be standing like a patient aunt while they shriek and giggle their way along the rails.

She's already told them that she's going to the art shop later. She doesn't want clothes. She's buying the Magic Pens set with the money Mum has lent her.

Apart from that, they haven't spoken much—or at least, not to her. They talk across her, sometimes trying to pull her in. But Taylor doesn't want to be pulled in. Soon they will see that this doesn't work. The gap between them is too huge. They can't go back in time.

"I've got a dress put by." Sam is talking to the stick-thin girl at the counter. She hands her a ten-pound note, and a ticket.

The stick-thin girl takes them, and scans the ticket briefly. Taylor notices she is wearing lime-green nail varnish. And her thumbnail has been filed back into shape.

The stick-thin girl disappears somewhere out at the back of the shop.

When she comes back she is carrying a dress. It's shimmery blue with black straps and tiny glitters of pearl woven into the silk. It has a jacket with it—cobwebby lace—the pearls sparkling through it like frost in sunlight.

The stick-thin girl glances at Sam. "Did you want to try it on again?"

"It's not for me," says Sam. "It's a present. For our mate."

Sam and Sophie turn to Taylor, grinning.

Taylor can't take it in. "I . . . you don't mean . . . you can't have . . ." Her voice is wobbling. Trembling.

"We got it that same day. That's why we made you wait outside."

"We pretended to look at those trousers, but really we went back to sort out the dress."

"We put a deposit on it and we've been paying for it in bits ever since."

"It's for the disco next week."

"You are still coming, aren't you?"

"We couldn't afford the shoes though."

"You'll have to borrow mine."

"Or mine."

"Or one of each."

Taylor lets them talk, coloured streamers wrapping round her. Bright. Colourful. Friendly. Safe. She doesn't speak—she can't speak. But she feels warm inside. As if the sun is shining all the way through her.

"Do you want to keep the hanger?" The stick-thin girl glances at Taylor. She is folding the dress, wrapping it in a sheet of pale lilac tissue paper.

"Yes, please."

The stick-thin girl lifts the dress gently and sets it

inside a silver carrier bag with a gold italic "Glitzie's" streaking across the outside. She hands it over the counter to Taylor. "And here's your penny change," she says.

49

"That was really wild," says Sam. "We have to celebrate."

"With a Coke and a burger," adds Sophie.

They walk back out into the precinct, Taylor holding the bag slightly away from her. She doesn't want to get it crushed.

As they turn towards the burger bar Taylor sees something—someone—by the water fountain. She hesitates. "You go on," she says to Sam and Sophie, "I'll catch you up."

She turns back.

Kat is sitting on the wall. There is a new scene beside the pool now. Snow White, her eyes opening and shutting, is laid out on a bed strewn with daffodils and primroses. A prince with eyes the blue of a warm spring sky is bending over her. On the plastic grass all around there are fox cubs and baby rabbits waving mechanical paws.

Kat hasn't seen Taylor. She is staring down into her own reflection, flicking ash into the water.

Taylor goes over to her. "Hello."

Kat looks up, startled. "Hey," she says. But her eyes are earth heavy. Taylor realizes that she was wrong about the smudged grey mascara. Mascara doesn't fade to yellowish blue.

"I just came to check you were okay."

"Why shouldn't I be?" Kat pushes her hand into her bag, and pulls out her cigarettes. "Fag?"

"No thanks. I'm just going for a burger and Coke."

Kat is already looking away, staring back down into the pool again.

Suddenly Taylor fishes her hand into the pocket of her vanilla cream jacket, and pulls out the penny change. "Make a wish," she says.

Kat takes the coin, rolling it between her fingers.

For a moment Taylor thinks Kat might just laugh, and hand it back.

But suddenly she stubs the cigarette out on the wall and flicks the coin upwards. It spins in an arc of gold through the air before dropping down into the water. Kat sits for a moment, very still, just watching where it has landed. Then she looks up at Taylor. "Thanks. See you around."

Taylor nods. "Take care of yourself." Then she turns, hurrying towards the burger bar, catching up with Sam and Sophie.